PARADISE:

In Search Of Love

SHARON HAMILTON

SHARON HAMILTON'S BOOK LIST

SEAL BROTHERHOOD
SEAL Encounter (Book .5)
Accidental SEAL (Book 1)
SEAL Endeavor (Book 1.5)
Fallen SEAL Legacy (Book 2)
SEAL Under Covers (Book 3)
SEAL The Deal (Book 4)
Cruisin' For A SEAL (Book 5)
SEAL My Destiny (Book 6)
SEAL Of My Heart (Book 7)

BAD BOYS OF SEAL TEAM 3
SEAL's Promise (Book 1)
SEAL My Home (Book 2)
SEAL's Code (Book 3)

BAND OF BACHELORS
Lucas (Book 1)
Alex (Book 2)
Jake (Book 3)
Jake2 (Book 4)

TRUE BLUE SEALS
True Navy Blue (prequel to Zak)
Zak (Includes novella above)

NASHVILLE SEAL
Nashville SEAL (Book 1)
Nashville SEAL: Jameson (Books 1 & 2 combined)

ISBN-10: 1945020474
ISBN-13: 9781945020476

AUTHOR'S NOTE

I always dedicate my SEAL Brotherhood books to the brave men and women who defend our shores and keep us safe. Without their sacrifice, and that of their families—because a warrior's fight always includes his or her family—I wouldn't have the freedom and opportunity to make a living writing these stories. They sometimes pay the ultimate price so we can debate, argue, go have coffee with friends, raise our children and see them have children of their own.

One of my favorite tributes to warriors resides on many memorials, including one I saw honoring the fallen of WWII on an island in the Pacific:

> "When you go home
> Tell them of us, and say
> For your tomorrow,
> We gave our today."

These are my stories created out of my own imagination. Anything that is inaccurately portrayed is either my mistake, or done intentionally to disguise something I might have overheard over a beer or in the corner of one of the hangouts along the Coronado Strand.

I support two main charities: Navy SEAL/UDT Museum in Ft. Pierce, Florida. Please learn about this wonderful museum, all run by active and former SEALs and their friends and families, and who rely on public support, not that of the U.S. Government.

www.navysealmuseum.org

I also support Wounded Warriors, who tirelessly bring together the warrior as well as the family members who are just learning to deal with their soldier's condition and have nowhere to turn. It is a long path to becoming well, but I've seen first-hand what this organization does for its warriors and the families who love them. Please give what your heart tells you is right. If you cannot give, volunteer at one of the many service centers all over the United States. Get involved. Do something meaningful for someone who gave so much of themselves, to families who have paid the price for your freedom. You'll find a family there unlike any other on the planet.

www.woundedwarriorproject.org

CHAPTER 1

I remember well the day John Gage stepped into my office. He had a whale of a tale about an island no one knew about, a white sandy beach with no telephones or internet, and a little thatched-roof bar tended by the most beautiful girl in the world.

He called it Paradise.

I hadn't even looked at his paperwork, or how much money he had to invest. I didn't look at what he did for a living. I just listened to him talk. His blue eyes and tanned skin, relaxed mode of operation, khaki pants, canvas slip-on shoes, and two or three day's worth of stubble all painted a picture of a guy who enjoyed life. Way more than I did.

The only remnant of his former life was the fact that he wore a button-down shirt, expensive one too, with his initials on the sleeve—if you were able to see them. He wore it wrinkled, right out of the dryer, or maybe off a clothesline somewhere, the cuffs rolled up to his elbows. He buttoned it one button too low, revealing a tanned and muscled torso. The guy was ten years older than I, but he looked ten years younger.

I was helplessly hooked.

It wasn't until after he left that I realized how much he'd deposited into his account.

"I want half of it in Treasuries. I don't care about the return. I want it bulletproof."

"Well, we hope the US will survive all the current turmoil and not go away," I said. "I think it's a safe bet."

"It is the safest on the planet. And you give me a plastic card in exchange. I like it. I can use that debit places I cannot use the cash."

"Cash?"

"Yes. No longer want to carry much. Just enough for a cheeseburger and a beer somewhere, or a taxi to get me to an airport, or someplace safe to sleep. That's all."

"Even taxis in New York City take credit cards," I reminded him.

"So I noticed. Even better."

"And the other half?"

"It gets split in two. Half of it goes to the Bank of Antigua, in a trust. I'll get you the paperwork in a week. Having it drawn up now."

"Okay. We hold off on that until you give me the authorization to invest."

"That's right." He smiled. Time was of no concern to him. Losing five or seven days of interest made no difference. He was making a change in his life. I could see that he was setting up a firewall to protect the rest of his days.

"So, we still have twenty-five percent," I said.

"In Swiss American National Bank, an interest-bearing account, staggered every month each with a 12-month call." He handed me two cards, each with a name of a bank manager.

"Interest accumulating?"

"Of course." His pearl-white teeth and sky-blue eyes were disarming. His face was nearly devoid of lines. There had been some there before, but it was like they were disappearing the longer I looked at him. His hair was streaked with some early gray, but feathered in with his normally sandy-colored locks, it was barely noticeable.

"Okay, so you've filled out the application, and I see a deposit slip."

John stood and extended his hand. "We'll talk in about a week when I get the paperwork from my attorney. By the way, Roger recommended you."

"Roger? Roger Sampson?"

"The one and only. Said you two were on the same SEAL team together years back."

"We were both snipers. Worked together during the crazy early days of the Gulf War and got out before they started slapping handcuffs on us."

"I'll bet you have some sandy stories to tell, as well," John answered.

I flinched. Hearing the term "wet and sandy" still made my blood run cold. "I saw all the sand I wanted to see in Afghanistan and Iraq."

"Blue water and palm trees?" he asked me.

"We practiced on them when we could, yes. So it was a different kind of experience. Sandy beaches are dangerous things in my past."

"Only thing dangerous about my sandy beach is losing your heart. Figuratively, of course."

"I get you. Good for you." I could see this had happened to him. "How did you get hooked up with Roger, if I can ask?"

"That's a funny story. I was actually reading an article on SEALs and what they did after their service. Roger was highlighted, doing intense and high-powered work for high net worth individuals. But he still had the ethics and tenacity of a SEAL. That worked for me. When I started accumulating my money and needed to set up a trust, I interviewed him over the phone. I've been happy with my choice so far."

"I'm glad it worked out, and you found your way to me."

He rose. "I'm off. See you in a few days. Thanks, Sean." He took his leave. I sat down at the desk and looked over the paperwork, stunned that I'd not gotten any details about him. I thought perhaps the new client information form would have something that would help me understand who my new client was. But, most of it was blank.

So I examined the deposit slip more carefully. I knew it had a lot of zeroes. I could see that. But I put on my reading classes to see how many.

My stomach fell to the floor when I realized he had indeed deposited ten million dollars today. I'd never seen an account opened with such a figure. I had very few clients with that size of an account, even after years of investing.

And all of it was in cash.

A week to the day, John was back in my office with the paperwork he'd brought from my former teammate, Roger Sampson's office. I'd been dying to have a conversation with Roger, just to ask questions about John and the source of the man's funds—if Roger knew.

I reviewed the header and was relieved to see Roger's oversized John Hancock-type scrawl on the last pages.

John was tapping his foot to some rhythm, flapping his hands on the padded armrests of my way-too-expensive, sky-blue, designer chair. His manner of dress was the same. Someone could have mistaken his fidgeting for nervousness, but I didn't pick that up at all.

"Do I have your permission to talk to Roger about your trust?"

"You can talk to him about anything you'd like— about my money, my plans, just don't tell him about my girlfriend."

"Your Ariel?" I felt I knew her, he'd talked so glowingly about her. The detail of how she walked, how her voice had that cadence and accent from the islands. I too felt like I could listen to her talk forever, just like John said.

"That's right."

I knew my face had scrunched up as I sorted his words. "Any reason why?"

"Oh, there are lots of reasons. He's got her name in there, so he knows that. He has the bare bones of her information, but since both of you guys are pretty darned Captain America-good-looking, I'm going to take the calculated risk of giving her contact information to you and you alone. Might as well diminish the odds that she'll leave me for one of you two."

I chuckled. I was recently separated from my wife of five years, a tempestuous relationship that never should have happened, and *wouldn't* have happened if I'd been deployed in the old days. But Roger was definitely a bachelor and was always on the prowl. I doubted he'd ever get married since he didn't seem to care for children, either.

"Well, John...if I can call you that?"

"Certainly."

"That attorney-client privilege is actually a tad bit stronger than our investment agreement."

"But the loss of your securities license would be a bigger deal. And do you ever read the paper? It happens every day."

"Well, I have a confession to make, John. I'm separated, soon to be divorced. Maybe that makes a difference in your assessment of me."

"Not one bit. I'm a good judge of character, Sean."

He told me more stories of how he'd met his mermaid, how he'd stumbled on the island. I wasn't sure I bought his entire story, especially the part about falling overboard on a pleasure cruise. I was sure no reputable operator would continue on and not go back and try to find him. I knew John's story was more fiction than reality. I hoped John did too.

He produced a map, showing a red circle around an area of blue water in the Caribbean Sea/Atlantic Ocean junction, between Barbuda and Antigua. He was right. There was no indication that any land mass existed there. In this twenty-first century, I didn't see how it was even possible.

He described the interior of the island as having a fresh-water pond coming from some underground artesian, with seasonal waterfalls erupting down the sides of a craggy extinct volcano top.

"So, how many inhabitants?" I asked.

"I'm not sure. There have been more in the history of the place, but right now, just Ariel's family lives there. I don't think any of them have ever ventured off the island."

"Really?"

"God's truth."

"So they own it?"

"Nope." John hesitated, then grinned and appeared to brace for a negative reaction. "I own it now. I bought it."

He flipped through his copy of the paperwork I'd provided, and then added, "I've made provisions for them to live on the island indefinitely. This money is for Ariel to run things, and pay for things if something happens to me." His eyes got a faraway look, and his smile quickly vanished, as if his whole body had gone flaccid.

I studied him as he picked himself up off his mental floor and pasted on a smile, the grin extending between his cheeks. But his eyes belied a touch of sadness. Maybe even a sudden flicker of fear, but then it disappeared just as quickly as his smile had evaporated earlier.

That was the first inkling I had that perhaps all was not completely well in Paradise.

I'd cleared my afternoon when I found out he was coming in this second time, so I just let him tell me as much as he felt like sharing. We went over the deposit agreements and federal funds rules. I noted that Roger had made note of the original account number, already opened, so we left that one intact and had all the other funds funnel into that main one.

"You have designated that Ariel is to get the balance of your estate upon your death. I'm sure Roger has forewarned you about the implications of your decision."

"Ah, but since when are affairs of the heart wise?"

"A few years ago, I would have said all the time. Now? Not so sure. But you have to be aware that there are beautiful mermaid sharks out there."

"Not my Ariel."

I wondered if he were just naïve or if he was in denial. No single woman could be that perfect. My skepticism must have shown on my face.

"You disagree?"

"I don't know her," I answered.

"Exactly my point." He leaned onto the desk and motioned for me to come forward, as well. He began in a whisper, "The woman has a heart as large as the blue ocean that surrounds her island. I would do anything for her. I have kissed every portion of her body, and I have found not one flaw. Her eyes see things I've never seen. She tells me the future and knows my past without me saying anything. I'm convinced *she* is the reason I've worked so hard all my life. And she's why I want to just go back to that island to live out the rest of my days. I'm going home to a family celebration, a wedding that will last for six days, according to the ways of her people. After that, she will be mine forever. That's the only thing I want to do now, return to Paradise and marry my mermaid."

John leaned back, and it took a few moments before I realized I was still arched forward, waiting for more. I'd never heard such stories, and was a bit ashamed to admit that I wanted to meet this woman, the mermaid of his dreams.

I'd been holding my breath again. Sitting back in my expensive, cushioned, orthopedic chair, I felt the leather caressing my skin as if the hide were still alive. I was sweating. My right hand had forced itself into a fist.

I'd been honest when I warned him about blind spots and mermaids, but I knew he wouldn't consider my cautionary remark for more than a second.

I was trying to bring myself back to reality, but I kept seeing vivid pictures he'd painted of this idyllic world of his. My desktop was cluttered with pieces of John Gage's future life. I spread my fingers and laid both hands flat. "Everything is in order, John. I'll prepare some instructions and draw up the paperwork for you to sign. You can come back tomorrow, or I can arrange for a power of attorney, and you could allow me to make the necessary filings on your behalf."

"That suits me better. I have one more trip up out to California, and then I'll be on my way. Make sure the debit card and my statements come to you, and then you can forward them to the address I'll provide you when I'm situated. Does that work?"

"Fine with me. You have temporary access checks here." I handed him the printed booklet with his name and my office address. "These are for your money market account. I didn't have a phone number to use."

"I don't need one," he answered, but gave me his cell phone for the record. "Texting also works. I have unlimited access."

"Very well. We are done, then."

We both stood and shook hands. I studied his tanned face, the lines of worry nearly eliminated now. I felt as if I would always remember John's confident smile. He was a man looking forward to the perfect life with the perfect woman in the perfect place.

"Be safe and let the wind guide you, Sean."

"Thanks. I envy you, John. I really do." I was surprised by my revelation, so unlike me.

"I know."

Two days later, I received a phone call from the Sonoma County Sheriff's Department. John's body had washed up on the coast near Bodega Dunes State Beach.

CHAPTER 2

Detective Watts Pecou appeared out of place as one of Sonoma County Sheriff's finest, he looked as if he should be investigating murders in his native New Orleans. His close-cropped, wavy hair was plastered to his head with perfumed pomade. His nails were buffed and lightly polished. His wedding ring sported an impressive diamond. He wore an expensive pair of silk slacks, four-hundred-dollar lace-ups that were probably Italian, and a stiffly pressed, tailor-made shirt that was probably from one of those mail orders in the Orient. His trench coat was the only thing that wasn't expensive, and I deduced that it was used on all his cases, especially when he retrieved bodies from rivers and from under bridges. He was an unusual creature of the night.

His slow drawl, piercing blue eyes, and coffee and cream complexion commanded one's full attention, and he certainly got mine. He looked as if he'd have been just as at home at any cocktail party amongst the firm's clients as he would be sampling fine wines in Paris or Sonoma Valley where he lived. But being from New Orleans, I bet he liked jazz and whiskey best.

"Y'all have quite a view," he said as he folded his tall frame into my expensive leather client chair. "You probably never get tired of it."

I chuckled because, after my separation from Corey, I'd actually considered moving out of the city into more modest digs, or perhaps getting a small farm in Connecticut and tele-commuting. I met with most of my clients on an annual basis, and I could arrange an office space for that.

His eyes pegged me as I got ready for our discussion. I saw he didn't miss a thing.

"You're right. I never do," I lied.

Pecou squinted then dropped his gaze to focus on an imaginary piece of lint on his trousers before he flicked it to the floor.

I found I was holding my breath again. With my SEAL training, I knew how to let it out silently without sending a ripple his way. But I knew he picked up on it anyhow.

"Detective, I took this job because my wife urged me to. She's a model, and this was more convenient for her. But no, I never minded the view."

"I understand," he said, nodding. "We gots to keep them happy. Those high-born fillies can be demanding." He winked at me. I knew he had never loved a woman like the type I had been married to, and that was okay.

"Needless to say, even that failed," I told him.

His eyebrows immediately rose, but I still didn't buy that he was surprised. "So, what we have here is an honest invest-ment advisor," Pecou said while leaning on my desk with one elbow, poking his cheek with three fingers of his right hand. His index finger was cut off at the first joint, and he wanted me to notice that. I'd seen worse, of course, but not sitting across a desk in an office that rented for a thousand dollars a square foot.

We stared into each other's eyes, and I can't say who blinked first, but something was understood after that moment.

"I guess John Gage's murder made quite a ripple if it sent you all the way out here to New York." I adjusted my head to watch him from another angle, not sure whether he was dangerous or just mysterious. One thing I did know...he was very smart, and anyone who underestimated him would do so at his or her own peril.

"Oh, yes. It was the big kahuna of the year so far. Barely made the paper, but it caught our sheriff's attention big time. He's an elected official in our part of the country. So that means something."

"I'll bet it does. So, what can I do for you?"

"Interesting you called it 'John Gage's murder.' You got a reason to believe it was murder?" He narrowed his eyelids, and his lips went into a thin, straight line. His eyes held no expression whatsoever. I imagined he could make the guilty feel guiltier just by the way he tracked them with his stare. He was like the Doberman my neighbor owned.

"Because your buddies told me he'd washed up on the beach. I know for a fact that he had a lot to live for, so I assumed he wouldn't commit suicide."

Pecou nodded again and seemed to be satisfied. "You know anything about what Mr. Gage did for a living?"

"He said he made money in real estate," I told him. Though I suspected the ten million in cash had a string that, when pulled, led to other things.

"Well, I suppose that's true, in a way. Did he mention anything about his farming business?"

I chuckled. "With all due respect, John Gage certainly didn't look like a farmer to me."

Pecou grinned. "Not your normal type of farmer. He never mentioned this at all to you?"

"Can't say he did. We talked about his girl and his island where he was headed. Not what he did."

Pecou considered my statement and carefully proceeded. "He was a pot farmer, Mr. Harper."

I sat back and watched the satisfying smirk on Pecou's face contrast with his twinkling, bright blue eyes that spelled excitement and dark, dark places I didn't want to explore.

"I had no inkling, no idea about that. He never mentioned anything."

Pecou nodded, his lips turning down into a half frown.

"I believe you. So, just how much did he invest with your firm?"

"I'm going to have to see some paperwork in order to release his confidential information. And I'm going to check with counsel."

"You do that. I'll forward the death certificate when I return to California." Pecou stood and looked out the window again. "Dang, that's a view a person would kill for."

"I didn't kill him."

The detective remained fixated on the Manhattan skyline. "I did some checking up on you already, and cleared you as a suspect. Your training in the Navy is most impressive." When he turned, he asked, "Did he leave a local address?"

I shook my head but double-checked the paperwork. "I think he stayed in a motel. I have his cell phone number here. I don't suppose there's any harm in giving you that."

"I got the phone itself. It was left in his place in Healdsburg. Plugged in to charge."

"Like he expected to come home and use it," I added.

Pecou gave me a stern warning with one eyebrow raised. "Exactly what I thought. You ever been to his place in California?"

"Nope. I didn't know him until about ten days ago."

"So where were the records being sent?"

"His statements? Here. He wanted them sent here."

"Curious," said Pecou.

It had seemed strange to me, too, but several of my clients who traveled preferred it that way, their financial statements sheltered from prying eyes. "People do it all the time," I lied.

"Next of kin?"

I flipped over the paperwork, and there wasn't any listed. "Just the girl on his Paradise island. Her mail goes to a box in Antigua. I don't think Paradise has mail service."

"A private island?"

"That's right."

Pecou faced the window again. "Mr. Harper, any reason Gage would fly all the way out here to New York to open up an account with you? Or have his will and other legal papers drawn up with your friend—he *is* your friend isn't he?"

"Roger Sampson?"

"Yes. The attorney. You two were chosen, and you're friends. Did you refer each other?"

"Roger referred Mr. Gage to me."

"So Sampson is the deceased's connection to New York, or is it something else?"

"Yes. He read about Roger in the paper. Roger referred him here. Like I said, I didn't know him that well, or for that long."

"Normally, someone picks an attorney or investment advisor in the state they reside in."

I shrugged. "I didn't get a chance to ask him for details, Detective. Maybe Roger knows. I believe Mr. Gage made Roger the executor of his estate. I don't believe John had any relatives, or none that made it into the will anyway." I'd put a call into Roger's office this morning before my meeting with Pecou, but hadn't gotten a returned call yet. I knew I would later in the day.

"Well, here's my card. Call me anytime. That's my cell." He pointed to one of the numbers with a 707 area code. "I'm not staying another night, going back on the red-eye. You'll call me with anything new?"

"I certainly will." I took his card, and we shook hands. I wanted to ask him more about the pot farming, but didn't want to appear too interested in the dead man's affairs—or at least more than I should be concerned about. But then curiosity overtook my better judgment.

"So, how does a pot farmer make that kind of money? Or are you saying that he did other things, too? I mean, isn't growing marijuana illegal?"

"Oh, not in California. People are making fortunes growing it for medicinal purposes and selling it to dispensaries all around the state. I believe there are five states now that have more or less legalized it for certain medical uses."

"So they can grow freely, then?"

"Oh, there's a boatload of regulation. Unbelievable how many permits there are. It takes over a year to get all the approvals, and it's expensive to set up. We have attorney firms springing up all over the place and that's all they do for people, get these set up. Not like you can just get some seeds and start growing in your backyard. But we understand that if done correctly, a person can make nearly a million dollars a year in sales from a small plot no bigger than an acre. That's a lot of change. But it also attracts a lot of bad guys."

"Wow. No kidding. I had no idea."

"I don't have to tell you the business isn't without risks. But if done right, and handled through a good firm, who helps match the grower and the landowner and sets up the lease and all the permits and paperwork, it can be worth all the hassle. Mr. Gage was one of the first to obtain his permits, and he was growing some very high-quality green."

"I wonder why he didn't use his California attorney," I mused.

"That's a very good question. Maybe he didn't trust any of them. You come up with anything, I'm all ears."

He turned to go, his wrinkled raincoat hanging off his shoulders like the cape of a disheveled vampire. At the open doorway, he adjusted his collar and gave me a short bow. "Y'all have a nice day."

CHAPTER 3

Corey had some function she needed me, even as her soon-to-be ex-husband, to accompany her to since most of our casual acquaintances thought we were still married. I wasn't in the mood. I thought about John and his island all evening as I showered, put on my tux, and then drove over to Corey's apartment to pick her up.

She lived in a place overlooking Central Park. Her modeling career had taken off big time, and to rub it in, she used another advisor from our firm to handle her money. The buck-toothed kid never failed to tease me at every company meeting, telling me how much she'd deposited into her stock account. But I always acted as if it was water off a duck's back, the smart thing to do—which, in fact, it was.

I couldn't get the picture of the beach on John's Paradise island out of my mind and watched as my imagination produced Gage's limp and pale grey body as it washed ashore. It was the wrong beach, not the rocky shore of Bodega Bay, which

I'd visited a few times in the past. But, somehow, I knew the island in the Caribbean was the reason for John Gage's death. His plans to leave California had somehow angered someone, enough to provoke his murder. I was certain his death wasn't suicide.

Corey was tightly put-together, wearing a long, butterfly print, organza jacket over white silk pants and a nearly see through, cream-colored shell. She always wore clothes that made a man look for wardrobe malfunctions, and probably left women wondering if she wore any undergarments. I knew firsthand that she usually did not.

Her flaxen hair was done up in a very severe twist with a wisp or two of curls hanging loose, begging someone to touch them and the flesh of her long, flawless neck beneath the tendrils.

She knew she was nearly irresistible, and I wondered why I allowed myself to be so humiliated, spending the evening with the woman who was going to be my ex, and doing so with a huge boner I could not control. Her little smiles and the whimpers at my side didn't help one bit. She would not let go of my hand so far this evening, and on more than one occasion, she placed it between her legs when she could get away with it.

"You haven't told me I'm beautiful, Sean." She had whipped right in front of me, so my forward step brought me slamming against her lean frame. I even felt her hipbones against my thighs. Her lips were so close to mine, I could have snuck a quick kiss, but I leaned back to avoid our collision there.

"Not like you to be clumsy. You have something on your mind, Corey?" I tried to sound casual.

She didn't move, so I stepped back. She grabbed the lapel of my tux and forced my face into hers where she planted a lip-lock that I was sure left red lipstick halfway from my upper lip to my nose. "I'm in need of a serious fuck tonight, Sean. And you're just the man to fulfill that need. You remember?"

Oh, my dick recalled very quickly and told me so, trying to tell her too, but I backed up again and removed myself from her clutches. I turned because I was afraid she'd paw me and find out I was stiff as a board. I was grateful that the tux had a generous cut to the trousers.

But Corey would not be deterred. In front of a roomful of whispering and glittering glass clinkers, she smoothed a hand over my ass and squeezed my left butt cheek, which made me jump.

"Good. I see you haven't let yourself go," she whispered and bit my earlobe.

I didn't like that she'd think I would let myself get out of shape just because she was no longer in my life. As a matter of fact, the opposite had happened. I felt like a young man of twenty again, free to date, and I was trying desperately to get all the negativity of my marriage to Corey out of my head. Roger sent me an endless supply of lovelies, so many that I couldn't remember their faces any longer. But everything had stopped about a month ago when one of my older clients asked if she could keep an apartment for me so we could go and fuck during lunch hours. I'd been a fuckin' Navy SEAL for chrissakes, and my negative reaction had nothing to do with her age or mine. I just wouldn't do that. In that instant, I knew how women who were offered the same thing felt.

Like a whore.

That's when I decided the city might not be the best place for me. Moving to the countryside in Connecticut sounded very appealing. In fact, I'd planned to start investigating that when John Gage entered my life.

I almost forgot that Corey was still behind me, pressing her mound against my butt and rubbing, one hand finding its way under my jacket to the beltline of my pants before I grabbed it and stopped the public display. No one was looking, or pretending not to see, but I made sure to squeeze her fingers hard enough that she quickly withdrew.

"I can see your stable of sex slaves isn't doing you much good, Corey."

With a *humph*, she whirled around and dove into the middle of the crowd and out of sight. The glittery masses closed ranks around her, then hovered and buzzed like a swarm of gossamer butterflies. These were not my people.

It was time to hit the little bacon-wrapped sausage specialties and caviar at the hors d'oeuvres table. I managed to snag a couple of the puff pastry spinach thingies presented by one of the glistening fairy servers with wings discretely tied to their collars. I was starving all of a sudden. The familiar slap on the back followed by the way his hand gripped my trapezius muscle told me Roger was here.

"How's it hanging, Sean?"

I made the mock gesture of examining my front side all the way down to my ankles. "Bigger than ever. It's a problem."

"You've been dodging some really wonderful girls."

"Really?" I couldn't recall getting even one call, and I said as much.

"Hmmm. That's not what I've been told," Roger spouted.

"From who? The woman who really wanted to bag you and not me?" I teased.

Roger winked at me. He studied Corey across the room, entertaining several white-haired men. "I don't have to tell you she's stunning tonight."

"Then don't."

"And I saw her working you. You'll cave, my little froglet."

I didn't like it when he called me that when we were on the Teams. I hated it even more tonight. Though we were in the same graduating class at BUD/S, he got his Trident just before I did due to his advanced rank, so he felt it forever gave him permission to exert seniority on me.

"Fuck you."

"No, thanks. But I think you and Corey could—"

I lost my cool and pushed Roger so hard he nearly fell backwards, instantly ashamed as I did. A woman screeched as Roger bumped into her, causing her to drench her chest with a nearly full glass of champagne.

Roger grabbed my arm and dragged me out onto the patio before any more attention could be drawn. Even Corey didn't have time to watch us leave the crowd.

"What the fuck's the matter with you, Sean? Since when do we not get to shoot the shit with each other?"

I instantly felt horrible. "Sorry, man. I think what's getting to me is this whole thing about John Gage. You get a visit from the detective from California?"

"He came to my office first thing. He's an odd duck, right? I think he has some kind of military background."

I was sure he didn't. "All street stuff, Roger. I'd stake my life on it."

"Well, he's different. Not what I expected."

"Got the N'awlins drawl."

"He does. He smells too nice for a cop."

"Detective, Roger. And that's the pomade he uses."

"He's a dandy with a wedding ring."

"He's more Columbo than a dandy. He's smarter than you think."

"What did he ask you?" Roger asked.

"Where Gage lived, what I knew of his business. Which reminds me, did you know he grew pot for a living?"

"Didn't have a clue. He did tell me that he'd sold his property in California. Was getting ready to just move off to some Paradise island. And while we're talking about it, I have to get some changes to his will done that he executed that last day he was in New York."

"What changes?"

Roger grinned, and I knew I was somehow fucked.

"Don't make me beg you for it," I said.

"Just read it over when I have the courier deliver it tomorrow. You'll see. Probably good that you didn't know today with your interview. I'm not authorized to give the police anything until they present me with a warrant."

"That's pretty much what I told him, too. I gave everything I could to the guy. But until he told me, I had no idea where John had gotten his money."

"Same here." Roger leaned forward. "You're being summoned.

I did a one-eighty and saw Corey coming right for me. "Hi, Roger," she said without even looking at my buddy. Her eyes remained fixed on me. "Come on, I want to introduce you to some people."

"Corey, I'm having a little confidential chat with Roger here. We have a mutual client, and…"

"Oh, nonsense. Haven't you guys gone twenty-first century? Why not do a Skype or Hangout tomorrow and catch up. Tonight, you belong to me."

In the old days, that would have been good news. Now, I rolled my eyes and allowed Corey to lead me by the arm back into the glittery crowd. I heard Roger chuckling as I left. I gave him a one-finger salute at my back.

At Corey's apartment, I handed the valet my car keys. Corey insisted I see how she'd redecorated her apartment for the third time this year. I was grateful my bank account wasn't being tapped for it. But Corey made double what I did, so she could afford all kinds of things I could not.

She handed the valet a twenty, and I nearly took it back.

"Way too much, Corey. I don't tip more than about five."

"So what? I do it to help him out, and he has a daughter, so he's saving for college. That's one thing that's different between the two of us. I care about people. You don't."

I didn't bring up the fact that half the planet would say it was the opposite. But I wasn't in the mood to argue. I'd killed people, and she, as far as I knew, had not. I wanted to be the dutiful ex and not inflame her more than necessary, at least to keep my legal costs down. I would look at her decorating and then go back to my place, shower for the third time today, and tuck myself into bed. I needed to be up at five-thirty for my early morning run.

Corey let me inside her twin carved mahogany front doors that she said came from a lumber dealer in Brooklyn and claimed had been recovered from one of the upscale apartments near the World Trade Center after the attack.

I barely heard the door latch before she was all over me.

"Corey—" I tried to speak, though she had her lips all over mine. Her breath was hot and laced with alcohol. She'd had a lot, which was often dangerous with her.

"Sean, I need a good fuck. I've been horny all day for you. It was so bad I had to bring my vibrator and—"

"Corey!" I screamed because she had her hand down my pants and was squeezing my balls. But it was no use. She wouldn't stop, no matter what I said or did. I resigned myself to just go with the flow.

"Come on, honey. I want you to be rough with me. I need it. Make me beg."

"But I don't like that."

"Pretend. Let's pretend you hate me and want to just fuck my brains out to get even with me for...for...kicking the dog."

That had me in stitches. I was laughing so hard, it was difficult to stay standing. My shirt was open, my bow tie undone and hanging, one side longer than the other. I could tell my hair was standing out in tufts because her fingers had wildly sifted through the strands, scratching my scalp. She'd pulled her jacket and top off, and had literally pressed her breasts— which were too small for my tastes—against my chest. She was working on my belt buckle. She stepped out of her pants once mine were at my ankles. I was amazed that she had gotten so far without any of my help.

"Come on, baby, fuck me," she said as she bent over, bracing herself on the divan in front of her as she showed me the creamy backs of her thighs and that perfectly round ass. It had always reminded me of a peach. I didn't bother to untie my shoes and be rid of my trousers, just bunny-hopped over to her quivering backside. When I touched her flesh, she arched and moaned. I squeezed her butt cheek, and she reared up into my groin.

"Get that big, fat cock inside me, Sean. Do it. Split me."

"Corey, how about a little foreplay?" I protested.

"Fuck foreplay. You need a pill? You already taking those to get hard, Sean?"

"Fuck no. I don't need no pill. Look at me."

She didn't look, just kept her backside rubbing into my groin, and grabbed my balls again, yanking down.

"Hoh! Corey, wait a minute. You're hurting me."

"Get your thing inside me, or I will really hurt you."

I used the anger I had to ram myself inside her, and the more I pumped, not being careful to make sure she was fully lubricated, just forcing myself deep and pressing against her cervix hard, the harder and bigger I got. Then I repeated the action over and over again until the frenzied pace got me winded. She was whining, moaning, and pressing back into me, spreading her legs wider and giving me full access. I'd never taken a woman this hard, and I regretted starting even before I finished.

My motions got more and more forceful until the divan began to move, scooting across the hardwood floor. The side table got displaced, knocking over the lamp on top, but we didn't stop. I knew the neighbors downstairs were probably being kept awake by all our noise, but Corey's shouting spurred me on. I wanted to possess her, turn her bones to rubber, and fuck her into the furniture. I hoped that after tonight, she wouldn't be able to sit down for a week, that's how hard I came at her. And yet, everything I gave her seemed to be exactly what she wanted. She even appeared to want more.

With my sweat transferring and blending with the trickle of sweat going down her spine, I bit the back of her neck where those little strands of curls had been earlier. I sucked, placing a huge hickey there, something she could be proud of.

But I wasn't. Her arch and hissing to the pain I had inflicted made me feel horrible. As the last of my seed filled her core, she held her breath and then sobbed.

Had I hurt her? I became alarmed.

Placing my hand on her shoulder, the other at her hip, I separated us, even as she continued to move back toward me. "Don't, please don't," she whispered.

"Corey, honey, I'm sorry. This isn't me. I'm so sorry. This isn't right."

"No." she whispered. "Don't...go."

"I'm done, Corey. Please, honey. Look at me."

This time, I made sure she turned. Her hair was completely coming undone, something I should have carefully done for her, placing her pins someplace instead of leaving her looking like some bride of Frankenstein with wires coming out of her head. Her cheeks were covered with tears, running mascara, and eye makeup. Her lipstick was smeared all over her mouth and up part of one cheek. Her eyes were vacant and desperate, watering from some craving inside her that had driven her wild but had sadly not been satisfied.

If I'd ever loved her, it wasn't tonight. This was not love. I was ashamed of myself for not resisting her. At that moment, I hated the city, this apartment, the sounds of traffic down below, the sirens and emergency alarms. I hated all the sounds of the busy life that I had created. I wasn't fed. This had not made me a better man, or a proud and worthy male.

I'd been robbed of my spirit. I vowed never to do this again.

What I really needed was what John Gage had found. I needed Paradise.

CHAPTER 4

The courier brought over Roger's package. Sheila, our receptionist, set it on top of the other Priority parcel in bubble wrap that had been delivered by mail this morning, as well. I'd just returned from making myself an espresso in the staff room and sat down to examine them.

Roger's papers were copies of the originals he had at his office. He had clipped them together with a personal, handwritten note on top. I always found it amusing to read the banner on his letterhead:

Roger Sampson, Esquire
Attorney At Law

When we were on the Team, I'd never expected to call him an *Esquire*. That was a magazine with some good articles, though not our tastes. We liked the ones with wet tee shirts and mud.

I'd never expected him to go to law school. Though I'd never expected to go into investments and securities, either, mostly because I used to spend my money as fast as I made it. But things changed, and we cleaned up well.

His distinctive scrawl on the piece of letterhead was barely readable, but it did look as if he'd made an effort. I could just hear his voice in the background as I read along:

Hey there, studly.

Don't want this letter becoming part of the client files, so toss it afterward, please, and keep your buddy out of trouble.

You'll note John Gage selected you as the executor of his estate. I advised him to do that, but he didn't listen the first time. Glad he did for our second meeting. I thought me being executor would be a conflict of interest, not that it stops some of our asshole colleagues. So, tag, you're it, motherfucker. That means you have to go on a scouting expedition to find his assets. A trip to California is necessary, but let me know if you want company. And I suppose you'll have to find the girl and get her the money she's supposed to get. All this will happen as they are investigating John's death, and I'm not sure what the insurance company will do, but I have a call in to them. You may have to take that over, too.

To compensate you, John left a salary of one hundred thousand dollars a year, plus reimbursement for your expenses. I've got the money in the trust account. Keep those expenditures tight and low, if you can. I will disburse to you monthly.

Be prepared for a distant relative to come out of the woodwork. In cases like these, the probability is higher than you think. Not accusing anyone of anything, but keep an open mind, and if you stumble across anything the detective should know, please tell me first, okay? We want to cooperate, but my job is to take care of the estate, and that means you as part of that. I don't want you to get your tit in a ringer.

Just like on our special ops, the Secretary of Defense will disavow any knowledge of this letter. Now burn the motherfucker and get your ass to California.

Oh, and while you're gone, is it okay if I bang Corey?

Yeah, that's what I thought you'd say.

—Roger

This was not something I'd expected, and now I was filled with apprehension that I'd be able to do this. Being an advisor was one thing, but working out his life plan and making sure I could pull in all the pieces of John's life, was quite another. And it was so unusual.

I looked over the sheaf of paperwork and all the attachments, including a copy of the blanket note John had taken back on the sale of the property, copies of closing statements and other back-up detail. I glanced at the Schedule of Real Estate Owned and saw the listings for several properties, including the island designated as just "Paradise." There was a small photocopy of the elevation of the island, showing the interior lake John had talked about, plus several deep valleys and outcroppings. A couple of springs were drawn in, and then I noticed that he'd divided the island up into four parts with initials in each of the quadrants, designating what I assumed were the areas where Ariel's family was located. Because of the size of the copy, the detail was missing and impossible to read.

I got out the map John left me and examined the little circle he'd drawn where his island was located. I wondered if it was indeed something a local would know about, and perhaps the reason it wasn't on the map was because it was too small and privately held. I knew diddly about this sort of thing, so I added the map to the clipped paperwork, did not discard Roger's letter as instructed, and set everything aside to examine the second package.

This one had been mailed from California and was addressed to me in John's handwriting. I tore open the plastic flap and found several copies of the same deeds from Roger's envelope, a copy of three closing statements, and a Bill of Sale for some farm equipment. He'd sold off high weed mowers, tractors, and other pieces of equipment with names I didn't recognize to Barney Colgrove Trucking. There were numerous other items in there, including some brochures for equipment, accompanying warranties, and some photocopies of permits for growing the medicinal marijuana, now transferred to the new owners: Barney and Jenny Colgrove. A preliminary title report was also enclosed.

And none of the amounts of the sale came to anywhere close to ten million dollars. It appeared John had sold approximately eighty-five acres, zoned "diverse ag."

I examined the settlement statement and found that John had carried a substantial part of the financing. There were two previous loans on the three properties that were paid off in escrow by the seller bringing in cash to close. That was a red flag. John Gage actually had to pay money out to sell his properties. I read over the blanket note that covered all three parcels and discovered that payments had been deferred for nearly a year, and the income was to be sent to Roger's address in New York City.

There was one property that was not sold. It was a house with a granny unit in Healdsburg near the town square, estimated to be valued at $763,000. It was free and clear, and there was a notation that the rent was $2,500 per month, payments to be made to John's trust account at Roger's office. I noted that the granny unit was listed as vacant on the schedule.

I knew one of the first things I'd have to do was get the house liquidated, so a meeting with the tenants—there had been a completed rental application in Roger's files—would be one of my first priorities. I'd have to find a realtor to give me an accurate appraisal of the property and negotiate with the tenants for the sale—if they were interested in buying.

I checked with my supervisor and was given the green light to leave next week on this new adventure. His executive assistant made all the plane reservations, as well as booked a room at a local motel. She set me up for a four-day stay. I figured everything could be wrapped up by then, and my ticket was refundable so I could change my dates without penalty in case I finished early.

Returning to my desk, I slipped John's packet back into the plastic bubble envelope. As I did, a photograph fell out that I'd somehow missed. It was a picture of a woman with coffee-and-cream-colored skin and curly dark hair framing a pretty, round face. Her eyes were honest, her smile unpretentious. She wore a bathing suit top and a sarong tied around her waist, and she was barefoot on a white sand beach. It appeared that the photograph had been taken with a cell phone and then printed. She was leaning against a pole with wooden signs showing miles and directional arrows to about fifteen cities and some countries across the globe:

Reykiavik
Oslo
Budapest
Prague
Paris
Berlin
Brazil
Warsaw
Bern
New York City
Healdsburg

She was pointing to the last sign, the one to Healdsburg. As I examined her closely, I could nearly see her saying something to me through the photograph, but I couldn't recognize the words. I could almost hear the sounds of the ocean pounding on the shore, and the clanging of metal grommets on the mast of a boat, even though the picture did not contain the image of a vessel. A small cluster of palm trees swayed in the background. The water beyond was bright blue, the color of Detective Pecou's eyes.

I knew this must be John's Ariel. Her wavy hair brushed against her brown skin, caressing her smooth shoulders. She looked part Pacific Islander, and part blend of Caribbean and European lineage. But she definitely appeared to be a woman of the world, that gentle mixture of magic and innocence of many nationalities.

And, somehow, she called to me.

I blinked, and the picture became stationery, flat, the image without movement. I turned over the photograph, and on the back, in John's handwriting, were the words, *My Ariel. Queen of my heart.*

I'd seen Corey dressed in her finery, Paris couture and the garments of runway fashion shows I'd been invited to as a special guest. I'd seen some gorgeous bodies, faces, and materials. But nothing I'd seen before matched the level of this innocent beauty. I knew right then that this would be a mission I would complete, no matter how hard the job. I would make sure Ariel received what John intended. I would follow his instructions to the letter.

For some reason, I brought John's packet home but left Roger's at the office. I made a light salad for dinner and elected to beg off the alcohol, getting rid of some of the overindulgences of the night before. There was a message from Corey on my phone, but I chose not to listen to it. I turned on some light jazz, took a shower, and put on my red, white, and blue pajamas that I'd taken with me all over the Middle East on deployments. Totally unnecessary, but they were like my security blanket on those dangerous raids and missions into unknown territories. Like traveling in outer space without a tether, I somehow felt happy and at home when I wore them, regardless of the real danger that lurked all around me.

The cuffs were tattered and beginning to fray, but nothing would make me turn them out to pasture. They were my favorite set of nightwear, and I wore them when I wanted to feel connected to my past. Tonight, I needed them.

I sat on the couch with a glass of ice water and took out John's files, setting the picture on top. I placed Ariel to the side and tried to look over the deeds and other items, but my eyes kept wandering over to the image. It began to move again, as it had in the office. This time, I tried not to blink, hoping to extend the experience, wishing for a revelation, and maybe some reward for my curiosity.

At last, my eyes got tired. I drank the rest of my ice water and went to bed. I saw Ariel's picture on the ceiling of my bedroom, her smiling face, her hair gently fingered by a Caribbean breeze. I heard a sea bird calling, and several others answer. The waves synced with the rhythm of my heartbeat. The salt air was refreshing, and the sun hid behind the fronds of several palm trees.

Ariel started to speak to me, but again, I couldn't understand her. Her face was close to mine as she bent down and whispered something to me before she kissed my lips. I extended my right arm and felt the warmth of her thigh beneath her sarong.

The island beauty's lips tasted like vanilla and sweet coffee, but her hair smelled like orange blossoms. She kissed the sides of my face, whispering in my ear little things I strained to hear. I saw the weight of her breasts bulging under the restraints of her top, and my fingers found a place to slip under the fabric to feel the fullness of her womanly orbs. My thumb caressed her nipple, and she smiled down at me, planting another kiss. I did not want the kiss to end.

She untied her top and unveiled her beauty in all its glory. Grabbing my hands, she placed them on her chest and allowed the goodness that was her warm flesh to overfill my palms.

I could feel my erection growing. She straddled my lap, and when she noticed the same, she giggled. I begged her with my eyes, unable to speak. She answered with another sweet smile, adjusted her skirts, and then took hold of my hardness with one hand as she guided me to her sanctuary. She raised herself up on her knees with the grace of an angel, and then came back down on top of me, her eyes closed. Her brow wrinkled as she moaned and slid over my length until I was fully seated. And then she rocked gently back and forth. My palms held her rear as she arched, rising and falling on my length. My thumb came around to the front and pressed her bud, and her eyes flashed open, her face beaming.

"You are perfect, Ariel," I finally had the words to say.

And then she was gone.

I tried for nearly an hour to re-create the vision of her making love to me somewhere on the beach, perhaps in Paradise. Had I transported there? Or, was this just a dream? But no matter how hard I tried, I couldn't retrieve her image again.

I lay back, feeling my dick pulse with need that would not be satisfied tonight. But my heart was filled with the promise that some day, though perhaps not in this way, I would meet John's Ariel.

CHAPTER 5

I extended the airplane seat all the way back to fully enjoy the first-class cabin accommodations I'd been provided. I made a mental note to tell Roger it wasn't my idea or doing. This wasn't anything like going "tight" as he'd requested.

Blue and white images floated in and out of dreams. I saw torches, heard the distant singing of chants, and felt someone's warm breath on my cheek.

When I opened my eyes, I found that the businessman next to me had migrated over the divide of the chair and was, in fact, breathing stinky alcohol breath all over the side of my face. I messaged the flight attendant, who gently woke the weary traveler and asked him if he needed some water. And, of course, he ordered another drink.

I put on my headset and listened to a calming new age station until I fell deeply asleep.

In my dream, I trudged through a jungle, the sounds of birds and unfamiliar insects buzzing in my ears. I was alone in this green cave of life. Were it not for the foliage, I may not have known where I was. But I was sure I'd gone back to Paradise. As I crested the gentle slope, I found a large lava rock to sit on and soaked up the breathtaking view of the turquoise water, the white, frothy surf, and the damp, cream-colored sand. The farther the beach was from the water, the brighter the grains were. I was without sunglasses, and my eyes hurt from the glare.

Standing, I continued my exploration of this amazing place.

I found a garden path winding through the jungle. It was a well-worn trail, more like the footpath of an animal of some kind. I was intrigued to find out where it led and was rewarded when a small thatched cottage appeared.

The jolting of the plane interrupted my dream, and I heard myself scream, but not in the waking world. I so wanted to go inside that cottage and investigate.

Now awake, the attendant motioned for us to put our seats upright and prepare for landing. My ice water was gone, as was the apple core I'd left on the tray table which I now tucked away. Just a few minutes later, we landed in San Francisco.

Detective Watts Pecou was waiting for me at the bottom of the escalator.

"Thank you for coming. I could have taken a bus."

"That's all right, Mr. Harper. This gives us a chance to talk. Besides, public transportation is loaded with seniors coming home from their vacations. Not your kind of crowd."

"I don't mind the elderly. We do have them in New York."

"Yes, you do. But we got this special breed of California senior. They're obnoxious as hell and so friendly, they try to start up a conversation with you, and then you can't get away from them."

"Sounds like you tried the bus a time or two," I added.

"Only once, and that was enough. First time I came out here."

"What brought you to California?" The carousel began to blink and beep as the baggage conveyor sprang to life.

"I followed my sister."

"So what brought *her* out this way, then?" I asked as I picked up my dark brown suitcase with my initials on it.

"That's a long story, and perhaps for another day. But let me just say it wasn't voluntary. At first, I stayed out here hoping to find her. And then I just remained."

"You mean, she was kidnapped?"

"In a manner of speaking. She followed this guy, kind of a cult leader she was introduced to at a revival in the swamp country. You know, like those television shows about the toothless guys who hunt gators?"

"Lovely."

"You get my drift. They was lowlifes. Somehow, they lost track of my sister, and, well, it got complicated. I haven't found her. Yet."

"Yet." We were walking across the traffic lanes to the parking garage. Pecou let me handle my own bag, probably knowing I wouldn't let him assist me. "How long ago was this?"

"Six years. I bugged the police so much, they finally gave me a job. I'd just graduated with a Masters in Criminal Justice"

"That's some story."

"It's all the truth. I never give up on anything. And I hate bad guys."

"Well, we have both of those things in common. My SEAL training helped develop that and beats out all the laziness and complacency."

"Which makes you hard to handle. I get it."

I winced and shifted my suitcase handle to my left hand. "I've been told that a time or two." I chuckled.

"You one of those guys who jump out of airplanes to take their blood pressure down a peg or two?" Watts was enjoying himself.

"Yes. I find skydiving relaxing. Beautiful, really."

"Well, I'm gonna take you at your word, then. Not a ghost of a chance I'll go up in one of those planes without a door on the side. No way. No how. End of story. Goodnight, Irene."

We approached a black, medium-sized SUV with lights discretely mounted at the back and front windows for emergencies. I hoisted my suitcase into the hatch in the back and climbed inside next to the detective.

"You hungry?" he asked me.

"A little. I slept through lunch on the plane."

"That's a nice flight, that non-stop from Newark. I've taken it a time or two."

He drove toward San Francisco's downtown and found a parking lot near the piers. It was a sunny and windy day, and the Ferry Plaza terminal was packed with tourists.

"This place has the best Chinese on the planet," he said as he opened a large door painted bright red. Inside, the hostess didn't appear to notice the detective at first, but then turned and ushered us to a tiny table in the corner with a view of the Bay Bridge.

"Is this acceptable, Detective?" she said in heavily accented but perfect English.

"It's perfect, Mai. Thank you, and thank Lin for me, as well."

"I will tell him so. Enjoy your lunch."

"Do you mind if I order for us?" he asked.

"Knock yourself out. I should pay, though, since you came all the way down here to pick me up."

"We'll see. If we get a bill, we can fight over it."

"So, you are well known in these parts."

"This was where they had that terrorist attack a few years ago, remember? The Chinese community has learned to appreciate law enforcement. I never have to pay for anything when I come here and shop in their community. Of course, I'm not a pig about it."

"I wouldn't expect you to be," I answered.

He ordered several dishes in a kind of pigeon Chinese, and the waitress stoically left us alone.

"One of my SEAL teammates was involved with stopping the bombing at the top of the Millennium. But you probably knew that."

"I wondered if you knew him."

"Not well. But he's now retired, running a winery with his wife up in Dry Creek. I'd like to pay my respects if I have time."

"I hope you do." He studied my face. "Zak Chambers. His wife's father was the chief of police up in Santa Rosa. Helluva guy, Allister Dobson."

Detective Pecou searched the crowd and found someone he knew, nodding in their direction. Then he turned his focus back to me.

"You have reservations to rent a car?"

"Not yet. Suppose I should have done that at SFO."

"Not necessary. I'll get you to the place we use when we need extra vehicles for visiting brass." He glanced down as the waitress brought something green with a side of some orange liquid. I must have frowned because he explained the contents. "This is for dipping. This is ground up fish, and this,"—he pointed to the green paste—"is made from eggplant and cabbage. I asked them to hold the horseradish."

It was a good thing, too. I didn't have the rotgut insides some of my SEAL teammates had. Even pepper sometimes disagreed with me. I was used to picking out onions and chilies from my dishes when I ate out.

"I've had Chinese in New York many, many times, and never had anything that looked like this, made from these ingredients."

"That's because this is all the rage here in California. Asian fusion. Like a combination of new age California-style healthy food with a heavy Asian influence. It's delicious, but I'll admit, different."

Mai brought us some fried wonton chips that were tasty all by themselves. I'd not realized how starved I was. I was glad I didn't have to venture into the territory of ground up fish and eggplant. It didn't look like it would taste good at all.

"So, first some ground rules."

I thought perhaps he planned to give me another lecture on the food, but then I realized he was talking about his investigation. I sat up to listen.

"I asked for a special favor, to have you tag along with me for a couple of interviews, since you're doing some investigating of your own. First, I had to tell my command that you were not a suspect."

"Wondered myself about that."

"You did? Good. I thought we could help each other out. But, Sean, you interfere with my team, my guys or my job, and I'll send you back to New York myself and it won't be first class either."

He didn't scare me. It was his way to reach out to me. I took it as a welcome, like the briefings we used to get in-country when on deployment.

"So you stay close. You don't talk to anyone unless I give you clearance, understood?"

"Sure. How come you get to operate like this?"

"Well, in case you haven't noticed, I look kinda different in these parts. Those in our law enforcement community know my history, and they also know that I mean only to go out there and bag bad guys. And don't get me wrong, I love my job."

"Good for you."

"So they let me do things a little different here. Not like in San Francisco, or New York, or even New Orleans. We're a little country. But when they see my face turn up, they know the job's gonna get done and I'm gonna get my man. I always do."

"Duly noted. I promise to be on good behavior."

"I got that court order for you, too, but I don't suppose you brought your brokerage records with you?"

"No. But if it's important, I can have things emailed or faxed."

"We're not exactly fast-tracking things. More interested in seeing what comes up. We're doing a careful investigation. So the ground rules are that you don't tell anybody who you are or why you're here unless they absolutely have to know. I'm going to introduce you as a special investigator from New York, and hint that you're FBI or ATF. But don't engage. This pot business has many facets, both in and out of law enforcement. Sort of like the Wild West. Going to take us a while to get it all sorted out."

"I got you. No problem."

"You don't go through any of Gage's things unless I'm there or one of my staff is on site to approve it. I don't yet know where or *if* there's a crime scene."

"I can live with that. I have to check into any statements or mail he might have gotten, try to find his checkbook and other personal effects. We have to find out how to get in touch with his woman."

"Woman?"

"He was moving to an island in the Caribbean. Meeting some woman there. I'm supposed to retrieve anything that pertains to his estate. Of course, I won't interfere with your evidence collection."

"Okay, we'll take it one step at a time. Slowly, okay?"

"Sure. Any suspects?" I asked.

"Not specifically, but my hunch is that it has to do with his cash crop. And even if I had suspects, I couldn't talk about that with you. We'll have to discover how to pass each other information, but do it so I don't compromise the investigation."

"Got it. So, if he sold his property, where did he grow the stuff?"

"Well, I don't think that matters now, do you?"

The obvious mistake I'd made was embarrassing. "So if he was making all this money, why did he want to sell?"

"That's a very good question, Mr. Harper. We knew he planned to leave. Though I'm sure he didn't plan on going out this way. Someone had a bone to pick with him, I'm guessing. Unless he just slipped and fell into the water. But I'm like you, I don't believe that one bit."

We continued talking while the courses of food kept coming. It didn't take long before I was completely sated.

"I'll get you in his place, although it's restricted because we haven't finished our search of the property."

"Sounds good. Where did he live? I only saw evidence of two pieces of property he owned, and one is in the Caribbean."

"The house in Healdsburg. He was living in the granny. But I have access to the main house, as well. The tenants are being cooperative."

"Good. Though when they figure out the place is being sold, they'll probably convert to enemies."

"Well, who knows? In this part of the country, the rich people don't dress rich. They drive old cars and wear mostly blue jeans and tee shirts. The only ones who dress up are tourists. Sort of the same way in the cities here."

I glanced at the crowd. It was a fairly young group, and Pecou was right. Most everyone wore blue jeans of some variety.

"Your buyer for that house might very well be the tenants."

CHAPTER 6

I picked up a rental car in Santa Rosa, a little convertible I imagined would be fun driving through wine country back roads.

I gave Zak Chambers a call. As a SEAL, he'd stopped a full-scale terrorist attack at a San Francisco landmark housing complex, and then was wounded on his first mission off the coast of Africa before he was medically discharged. I figured I'd stop by to pay my respects. I'd trained with their group but was already scheduled to disengage from SEAL Team 3 before their mission to the Canary Islands. Though I was dying to know if Zak knew anything about my former client.

He'd invited me over for dinner, so after a picturesque trip up from Santa Rosa, I got situated at the little boutique hotel on the square, took a quick shower, and then headed out Dry Creek Valley to Frog Haven Vineyards. With the top down, the beautiful green rows of vines contrasted with the blue of the cloudless sky and made my heart sing. I was so glad to be out of Manhattan. I hadn't realized how cooped up I felt. The less I heard the sirens and traffic, the more relaxed I felt. It was my own little piece of paradise, similar to what I imagined John Gage had felt.

It struck me as odd that he'd want to leave all this behind, but then I remembered his Ariel. She was the magnet. I knew he was running away *to* her, and hoping never to be found again. But was he also running away *from* someone else? Or maybe some situation. That seemed to be the most logical explanation for why he'd become a target.

The tree-lined, crushed granite driveway was barely big enough for a large truck, so when one came barreling around the corner, windows rolled down, blaring loud mariachi music, I was barely able to stop in time. The driver, wearing a battered straw hat, veered off into the vineyard and waited for me to pass. My heart was in my throat. That had been a close call.

A little bungalow with a welcoming, wraparound porch came into view. Four rocking chairs were positioned there, two on either side of the front door. I parked and made my way to the entrance.

Before I got to the landing, a pretty, young, blonde woman carrying a baby greeted me.

"Sean Harper?"

"The one and only. You must be Amy."

"That's right, and this little one is Keira."

The chubby toddler extended her arms, and I was suddenly holding the squirming youngster, trying desperately not to drop her. Keira changed her mind, and I was only too happy to return the girl to her mother.

"Zak's out in the field, but I'll let him know you've arrived. I hope you're hungry."

"I had a huge late lunch, so no promises."

The old living area of the house was set up as a wine tasting room and showroom, where tourists could purchase tee shirts, snacks, bottled water, and wine, as well as picnic baskets and implements, including wine country cookbooks. I noticed they also sold beer.

"Beer? At a winery?"

She laughed. "Lots of places are doing the small microbrewery thing now. Very popular. We're going on our second season with our own hops. This whole area was once prime hop growing territory for the breweries that used to be in San Francisco. When the brew houses relocated out of the City, wineries and fruit orchards took over. We like to think we're coming full circle."

She held up a growler with the label, *Frog Piss Beer*. Keira was aiming to grab the brew right from her mother's hands, and Amy had to twist to keep it safe. The label had symbols I well recognized: the bone frog with spear and the Navy SEAL Trident. "I've definitely got to get one of these." I lifted another six-pack of *Punish Me* beer with the Punisher skull that SEALs knew well. It was the most common tat any SEAL wore, other than the bone frog.

"Come on into the kitchen, and I'll pour you one. Unless you'd rather have wine," she said.

"I'm dying to taste this." I held up the green *Frog Piss* growler.

I followed her and sat at the counter where she directed. She put Keira down in a playpen and gave her a rattle toy, then made her way over to the small keg in her refrigerator.

"So, you're here doing some research on a client of yours back in New York?"

"His name was John Gage."

She shrugged. "Don't know him," she said, her back turned.

"He actually lived in Healdsburg."

"*Lived?*"

"Unfortunately, he was found dead up at Bodega." I remembered Detective Pecou's admonition not to discuss the case, but I figured her lack of recognition when I spoke John's name was a safe signal.

"That's terrible." She handed me a frothy beer mug with the most beautiful amber liquid I'd ever seen. I took a large gulp and set it back down between us.

"Ma'am. You're mislabeling this stuff. *Frog Piss?* This stuff is the elixir of life."

She grinned just as Zak Chambers entered the room. He wore a black patch over his lost eye. The injury was the reason he had been discharged, though he had requalified as an expert on every firearm, proving he still had the ability to serve. But in the end, he'd decided he was a liability to his brothers and was later released.

"Hey, Sean. It's been a while."

We did the obligatory hug and slap on the back, and then the handshake and knuckle-busting.

"Gosh, Zak, for the life of me, I cannot figure out why you'd want to stay here in this ugly place. Wouldn't you rather get shot at and risk your life every day? Eat dust and sand for breakfast?"

Zak examined his feet, and I could see I'd hit a sore nerve. Amy came over to him and placed her head against his chest, her arm around his waist.

"He wanted to stay in. He would have, wouldn't you, Zak?"

She looked up at him admiringly. Zak bent down and kissed her. "That ship has sailed. On to our new adventure here," he whispered and kissed her again.

The baby was standing at the wall of the playpen, seeking attention from her dad, her arms outstretched. Zak pulled her up to his chest and rubbed noses with her until she giggled and squirmed to be let down again.

"So, did you ever meet a guy named John Gage?" I asked him.

"A Team guy?"

"No. He was a client of mine."

"They found him dead, Zak. Remember the guy they found at Bodega Dunes? I think that was him." Amy had poured Zak a beer.

"Oh, you know, I do think I met him one time here. I recognized his picture in the paper."

Amy was alert.

"He came here with a bunch of other guys. Definitely not Team guys. A little rough around the edges. It was more than a year ago. We talked about the Teams. He had a lot of respect for the SEALs. His friends were clueless."

"So you're here to help them investigate?" Amy asked.

"Actually, I'm not supposed to say anything. But I figured I could trust you two. They don't have any suspects yet. I'm just nosing around, but really what I'm doing is gathering his things together. I'm the executor of his estate. But Detective Pecou thinks I might run across something if I keep my eyes and ears open."

"We're good. No worries here." Zak took another sip, engrossed in thought. "I'm trying to think who I saw him with, or anybody else who might have known him." He looked up at me and smiled, which made his eye patch bulge. A true pirate. "I'm coming up blank. Sorry, Sean."

"Well, I'm just here to pay my respects to you and bring greetings from Roger and me. You remember Roger Sampson? He left just a little before I did."

"Team 3, as well?"

"Yup."

Zak shrugged. "Sorry. I don't remember him. I was pretty green back then. Amy and I had re-connected after some years of separation, and boy was I distracted in those days. Plus, we'd just had that terrorist thing in San Francisco where she was working. And I was headed out to my first mission. I had a lot on my plate. Perhaps it contributed to…" He touched his eyepatch and then shrugged again. "But life moves on, and I'm all settled now. I see flowcharts and chemical equations and sales figures in my sleep. My fingers are permanently stained purple. I've never worked so hard in my life, but we love it. A bunch of the Team is invested here, too, or perhaps you knew that."

"I did."

"Well, keep it in mind for your rich clients. We have a limited partnership here, but we can always use the additional capital to upgrade our equipment and get other acreage under contract for production. We always need funding, even though we're,"—he held up his fingers to show a nearly infinitesimal amount—"this much in the black."

"Black is beautiful. Stay in the black. You can't go wrong there," I answered.

After enjoying a leisurely dinner of pasta and fresh salad from their vegetable garden, I said my good-byes and drove down West Dry Creek to the square. It was a nice lifestyle here in Healdsburg. Next to my hotel entrance was an ice cream shop, so I indulged in some rich, hand-churned French vanilla ice cream topped with homemade caramel sauce. I knew before I left the shop that I'd be comatose in an hour.

My room had a full refrigerator-freezer in it, so after only consuming half the small batch of ice cream, I stored it in the freezer for tomorrow night.

I sat at the padded bench seat in front of the tall, narrow window overlooking the square, observing couples passing by. Little kids played, and grandparents sat on the park benches and observed the crush of traffic like I did. Zak had said at night he saw figures and pie charts and chemical equations having to do with his wine making. I used to see bar charts and ticker symbols in my sleep.

But as I slipped on my red, white, and blue pajamas, I decided to turn in early. And, staring at the ceiling again, there was Ariel. I tried not to blink for as long as I could hold out. I willed her to come to me again, to warm my body with the smooth mounds and valleys of hers. I wasn't going to say a word. I would lay back and enjoy whatever she brought me.

I hoped the fantasy with "Ariel would stay forever. I knew exactly how John Gage had felt.

I felt the same way.

CHAPTER 7

I met Detective Pecou early the next morning over break-fast and very strong coffee—the kind that would make New Orleans proud and would likely keep me going to the can all day. The diner up the street was known as the best lo-cal place for breakfast. No one ever finished the large plates served with heaping piles of cottage-fried potatoes and west-ern scrambles or five-egg omelets. The platters were so heavy, our waitress brought them one at a time.

Again, I was hungry. My body seemed to have used up all its fuel and was craving more. I considered our late lunch at the Red Door in San Francisco and wondered if the "fusion" food had actually uncorked something in my system. I was dream-ing like never before, consuming large quantities of unusual food groups, and still feeling starved and wanting more. I slept like an old dog in a sunny window. Driving around Sonoma County instead of being cooped up in my beautiful Manhattan office was clearly very good for me. Something about the whole adventure and the mystery surrounding my new former client ignited the inner sleuth in me. I felt a pull and a calling to do something extreme, exotic, and exciting.

I hadn't felt this way since the day I left the Team. Sure, I'd known I couldn't be a SEAL my whole life. I envied those guys who found a spot and could stay serving the Navy and put in twenty or twenty-five years. But, like most men, I couldn't do that. I mean, my *body* couldn't. On cold days, my left ankle hurt, and my left knee would probably need to be replaced by the time I was forty-five. I'd broken every long bone in my lower body at least once—some twice. I'd broken ribs. I had deep gashes and scars on my fingers, and my pinky finger on my right hand would never behave, causing some of my buds to call me "MiniMe," tossing the Mike Meyers' classic gesture of the little finger in the air when they were trying to get my goat. With the ladies, I could always make up some heroic or frightening tale, depending on whether or not I ever wanted to see them again. My scars and injuries were part of the stuff that made me the man I was. They were also reminders of days past when I lived for it, breathed it, and nearly died for it.

And the plain truth was, I missed it.

This new, energized mission into the unknown provided that same kind of feeling. It was part folly, part imagination—especially the dreams—part anticipation, and part just good, plain old adrenaline. As I cozied up to recreating John Gage's life, retracing his steps and beginning to accomplish the job that he'd started, I suddenly felt more alive and energized than I had in years. Even all the years bobbing and weaving, sparring with Corey—which at first was kind of fun, playing with a woman who was demanding and all-inclusive—were not as exciting as this new adventure. Corey had gotten me adjusted to being off the Team with the distraction of her downright sexual energy. But when that faded, and it became something that made me feel ill inside, there hadn't been anything to replace that desire to be crazy and risk it all.

Until now.

And, just like being on the Team, it made no sense. It *shouldn't* be exciting getting your ass blown up, or possibly coming home in pieces, or worse yet, coming home in a box. But damn, it was. It was all that and more. And being able to play with all the other crazy-ass men who I served with—well, there wasn't anything in the world like it. No one understood us at all. They might pretend they did, but they didn't.

I became aware of the fact that Detective Watts Pecou had stopped eating and sat across the table from me, his utensil clutched in his right hand. He just stared. The forkful of cheesy-spinach-onion-mushroom-jalapeno scramble was piled so high, I was concentrating on balancing it so I could get it to my mouth without spilling it all down my front. I'd inhaled and glanced up at him with my mouth ready to accept a Mac truck when I noticed his reaction. His eyebrows were tightly packed up into his hairline, his blue orbs twinkling with a look somewhere between concern and horror.

I quietly lowered my shovelful and cocked my head, my palms gestured to the sides. "What?"

"Take a look at your shirt, man."

I dropped my chin and noted the drips of wet butter and bits of egg stuck to the surface of my shirt. My jeans were covered in crumbs, too. As I looked back up at him, I became aware of the dribble down my chin, also peppered with eggs.

"You always eat like that?" He finally revealed laugh lines at the sides of his eyes, and I relaxed a bit.

"I was thinking." It was the God's honest truth.

"Were you even conscious of how much you were piling into your body? I've never seen anyone do that. Even at a hot dog eating contest, and that involved a lot of barfing afterward."

I grinned. I'd been caught, fair and square. "Don't judge me too harshly."

"They train you guys to eat like that?"

"That's not all they train us to do," I said, wiggling my eyebrows up and down.

"Don't go feeding me that horseshit. I got enough problems. Now I have to picture you going all Captain Commando in the bedroom, too?"

Detective Pecou had attracted some attention nearby, and a mother with her two children folded her hands over her little girl's ears.

"Sorry, ma'am," he said as he nodded respectfully in her direction. But then I heard him whisper a filthy string of words while shaking his head. So much for making a good impression.

"Can't take you anywhere. You always do that?"

"I don't know. Watts, my man, this is only our second date."

"Fuck this." He stood and tossed his cloth napkin at me, and it draped over my medium-sized shovelful of potatoes. "I'll be outside. Gotta have a smoke."

The family next to us watched him leave and then examined me. I gave the little girl a nice wave, and it appeared she needed permission from her mother before she would return it. Her mother didn't encourage her.

Pecou had not paid the bill, so I figured Gage's expense account could do the honors. I tipped the waitress generously and requested a to-go cup for the delicious black coffee, then changed my mind and asked for two.

Pecou's trench coat was tangled in the breeze as he stood on the sidewalk, inhaling his electronic cigarette. The coat was in even sorrier shape than I remembered it being in New York. I handed him the cup, and he thanked me with a frown.

"You trying to quit, or do you like it better?"

He looked at me cross-eyed. "I just might toss three months of abstinence out the window if I keep hanging around you." He took a sip from the cup and put away his device. I knew better than to ask again. That information was on a need to know basis, and I definitely wasn't on the list.

I decided to ask one more thing and see if he'd recovered. "You expecting to see a dead body today, Detective? Kinda hot for a trench coat."

"So now you're the fashion police, too. What else the fuck do you know how to do to irritate someone? I'll bet your woman has some stories."

"She does. She definitely does."

"I wear my trench coat sometimes because it has pockets, and I keep my evidence bags in them." He demonstrated by pulling out the plastic bags from a deep side pocket. "I got pens of every color," he said, opening up his lapel, revealing a row of permanent markers clipped to a pocket protector for safekeeping. "And then there is room for other things, too." He showed me his brass knuckles, his handcuffs, two clips for his sidearm, a set of latex gloves, and plastic goggles to protect his eyes. All this was in the other large pocket on his left. "Think of it as a lab coat." He grinned and made a sweeping motion through the air with his fingers, indicating that he meant the whole area in front of him. "And, this is my lab. Welcome to my world."

I didn't say anything for a bit, then decided I'd make nice. "Can I call you Watts now, or is it still Detective Pecou?"

"Detective Pecou."

"Okay great, Detective. So then I take it you're going to need backup. I'm here to do whatever you want me to do. If we're bagging things, you just tell me, as long as I am allowed to do it. If we're examining blood splatter patterns, and you want me to take a picture, just tell me where to point and click. If I need to tackle someone, just give me a whistle. I'll be your Huckleberry. If we're gonna see a dead body, you might get the reappearance of all the breakfast I inhaled this morning. I've never stopped being disgusted by what a dead person looks like."

"Well, aren't we a pair, then? Let's get over to Gage's studio and let me put those considerable skills to work, Frogman to the Stars."

CHAPTER 8

Gage's house on Matheson Street was one of the smallest homes in a row of substantial, turn-of-the-century, painted ladies with beautifully manicured front yards. Behind well-maintained white picket fences, each lawn was an explosion of blooms, looking like each was trying to outdo their neighbor. The house was well kept, but it was about half the size of the mansions. And, instead of a big back yard with a pool, this dwelling had a granny unit tucked under a walnut tree, barely visible from the street. In fact, if we didn't know better, we might have mistaken it for a tool shed or workshop.

We climbed the steps to the beveled glass front door framed in solid oak and carved in a vineyard motif. Pecou turned the brass doorbell handle that reminded me of a bicycle ringer, and in seconds, a very pregnant young woman answered. She was attractive, or could have been, but she'd clumped her hair on top of her head with a clip and wasn't wearing any makeup. Her large belly protruded over the drawstring waistband of what I recognized as a man's set of pajama bottoms. She wore a sports bra, which would not be of much use shortly as she spilled out the top in an eye-catching display of heaving flesh. I knew it was probably just as hard for the detective to ignore her mammaries as it was for me.

"Ma'am. I'm Detective Watts Pecou," he said, extending his card. He focused on his fingers, shaking a little, holding on to the gift, but I saw the quick peek at her chest I was sure he tried to hide.

"Who are you, then? You have a card?" she said, turning to me. I detected she wasn't a very nice person. I knew better than to tell her I was the man who was going to make her move, that is, unless she happened to have seven hundred something thousand dollars in her back pocket. But John had brought in ten million without any fanfare, so I decided it was possible.

"I represent the estate of John Gage. I'm Sean Harper." I extended my hand, and she ignored me, speaking to Detective Pecou instead. "So, he's an attorney, then?"

"Ah, no, ma'am," he said as he glanced over at me. "He's an investment broker from New York. Out here to help Mr. Gage settle his estate."

"But he's dead."

Neither of us missed the fact that she didn't appear to be a fan of Mr. Gage's.

I decided to lend a hand. "I'm here to carry out his wishes. He appointed me executor of his estate."

She hung her head to the side and gave me bored attitude. "When are you putting this house up for sale?"

"I don't have an answer for you yet, ma'am." Since the horse was out of the barn, I decided to proceed, but cautiously. "But I'd start looking for a new residence, just to be on the safe side. Moving—"

"Well, I'm not. I got rights, and I have a fucking great attorney I've already talked to, so don't try to pull any of that New York City bullshit on me. I'm staying here as long as I feel like it. And if I get harassed, I'll just take this big pregnant belly to the judge and tell him what a mean man you are. Does that just about sum up my position for you, sir?"

The woman wasn't afraid of anything. Or she was very naïve. My knowledge of real estate was limited, but absent being in some rent-controlled city like San Francisco or New York, there wasn't a whole lot she could do. Landlords had rights and certainly had the right to request a tenant, even a long-term tenant, to leave, as long as the rules were followed. But if I tried to force her to move, or make her leave faster than she wanted to, I'd be frustrated. She'd be difficult, and she could use her pregnancy as a defense.

"I don't blame you. Must be hard in your condition to be contemplating a move. Totally understandable." I meant it, too. "We'll make sure we take it slow, and one small step at a time."

"Okay, but get ready for a battle if you don't."

"Don't what?"

"Don't move very, very slow. I'm sure we can agree on a timeframe somewhere between the birth of this little munchkin and his leaving for college, Mr.—what was your name again?"

"Harper. Sean Harper." I swallowed hard and turned to the detective, indicating that I was done talking to her.

"So, Mrs. Bromley—"

"Miss Bromley. I'm Carla. You can call me Carla. My old man is at work. He's Lewis Grebe."

"Okay, Carla. When we talked on the phone, I mentioned that I'd like to ask you some questions about John Gage. May the two of us come inside?" Pecou knew how to play nice better than I could at the moment. The woman had nearly shot down all my defenses and done so without fear, which was even worse.

Her eyes flashed to mine immediately. I would have thought she would be more concerned with Pecou. I wasn't an authority figure. I was a layman. She nodded and stepped back, allowing us to enter.

She had Joni Mitchell music on. The house was not well kept. A pile of laundry covered the living room couch, where she had apparently been folding it. I smelled the distinctive aroma of pot once I came farther into the space. Pecou must have noted the same.

"Are we alone here, Carla?" he asked.

"Just us chickens."

"Okay, may we take a seat?" He pointed to one of the chairs in the living room, not covered with laundry.

"Sure. Let me get rid of this." She picked up an armful of clothes. I went over to help her, but she declined. "I'll be right back."

When she returned, she turned off the music, took the couch, crossed her legs, and addressed Pecou. "Your questions?" The woman was all business. She didn't offer refreshment, indicating she didn't consider this much of a social call, so she wasn't going to try very hard. We'd have to pry information out of her with a crowbar. It was time for Pecou to show what he was made of. I would stand back and observe, perhaps learn a thing or two.

"When was the last time you saw Mr. Gage?" Pecou asked.

"He's been gone a lot. Probably a couple of weeks. Maybe more."

"Has anyone come around looking for him?"

"You mean other than the cops? No. He used to hang out with some of Lewis's friends, but not lately. Pretty much stuck to himself for a long time now. The past year at least."

"Were you aware what Mr. Gage did for a living?"

"You mean grow pot for the dispensaries? Yeah. We all knew it. He was cool with us smoking it, and we were cool with what he did. Not the details, of course."

"Do you know where he grew it?"

"Oh, geez, someplace west of here, I think. Lewis knows. I never talked to him about it. Just, you know, overheard things."

"Anybody who didn't like him? Did he have enemies?"

"Well, before he became a hermit, he was always friendly. Decent guy. I can't imagine anyone not liking him. He was cool when we had a problem with the rent. Never got heavy with us. I just think he was making so much money, what we were paying him was a drop in the bucket. He didn't seem to care much about cash. If we had a problem, he always got things fixed. Couldn't ask for a better landlord."

I wondered if Pecou had the same reaction to her oversharing about what a nice guy Gage had been as I did. The obvious elephant in the room was that someone had succeeded in killing him.

"So what caused the change? When you say he became more like a hermit, anything you can think of that might have caused that? Women problems? Issues with his pot farm?"

"God, beats me. I never saw him with a woman. Ever. I mean, no one he brought over here. We'd have known."

I noted that she'd left off the part about business problems.

"So, when you say he was like a hermit, in what way? How did he act before and then after, and can you remember when this was? All of a sudden? Gradually?"

"Like I said, it was about a year ago, maybe longer. I was like 'I haven't seen John around,' and that's when I realized he'd been gone a lot more. He was just never here. Before that, we'd see him all the time, getting in his truck, hauling things to the dumps. He'd offer to take our stuff, too. We never had any deep, meaningful talks with him or anything. But I guess it was fairly sudden. He was just here one day, and then he was gone. He'd come back for a couple of days, and then he'd be gone again."

"Did he explain himself?"

"Not to me. Lewis saw him more than I did."

"Did he ever offer to sell or give you any of his crop?"

I could see she didn't want to answer this question.

"I was smoking weed long before I learned some of it was from John's stash. It was...*is* some good stuff."

"Did he acknowledge he'd given it to you?"

"I never talked to him about it. Lewis got it from him. John and I never talked about what he did. Lewis told me."

"Were Lewis and John close at all?"

She shrugged. "Not particularly. Toward the end, he had become a very private person. Like he just pulled away. Became indifferent. He wasn't even interested in the baby coming. He was distracted."

"When can we talk to Lewis?"

"He'll be home tonight, but late. Come back around ten o'clock for the best chance of catching him before he hits the sack. If I know you're gonna call, I can keep him awake until that happens."

"Fair enough. So, you have keys to the cottage?"

This surprised me. It certainly wasn't typical behavior to give keys to the complex to a tenant. If Pecou thought it was strange, he surely didn't seem to be concerned about it. That took her off my mental list as a suspect unless John Gage was as dumb as a box of rocks. And I didn't think he was dumb at all. Maybe a bit delusional.

She opened a drawer in the kitchen and rummaged through several things in what sounded like a junk drawer, then brought out a set of keys on a fob in the shape of a truck.

"Here you go."

Pecou examined the plastic key fob. "Barney Colgrove. He a friend of Gage's?"

"Not really. Just some dumbass local guy. Lewis has all the skinny on him."

It sounded to me like Lewis was the one we really needed to talk to. Pecou gave me a half smile and then asked, "You got any questions for Carla here?"

She aimed her attention on me like a large cat ready to pounce on the mouse I was perhaps trying to protect.

"Have you met Barney Colgrove?" I asked.

"Yes."

"Over here?"

"I don't think so."

I wasn't getting the overshare. I was going to have to work for it.

"So, who is this guy? A trucking contractor? Did he work for Gage?" Pecou asked.

"I'm not exactly sure what he was to John."

When I saw Pecou quickly raise his chin and examine Carla's face, I knew he caught the reference to Mr. Colgrove in the past tense. Were we about to find another body?

"Any idea where we can find him?" I asked.

She pointed to the keys dangling from Pecou's fingers. "There's a phone number on there. I'd give his office a call. Maybe his dispatcher knows."

I knew we were on borrowed time. It was going to be a long day if we had to come back at ten. After the huge breakfast we'd had, I needed a nap, and fairly quickly. As well as a stop at the restroom.

We were ushered out the same way we'd entered. After the door had slammed, we heard the muffled sounds of the Joni Mitchell music return.

Pecou walked fast. He fidgeted and grimaced like he was constipated. I certainly wasn't.

"Would it be possible for me to use the bathroom in the cottage?" I asked.

"Nope. You're gonna have to hold it or go see Miss Bromley about it. I'm not going to mess anything up here. And you're gonna need to wear these." He handed me a pair of gloves.

He glanced down at my slip-ons. "Leave your shoes outside the door and go in with only your socks on, okay?"

"Roger that. You're lucky I'm wearing them today. Most days when I'm on vacation, I don't."

He shook his head. "You frog boys. Ain't you somethin'? You probably go commando, too. That means—"

"I know what it means, and you're very perceptive."

"So you consider this a vacation, then?" He was focusing on getting the key into the lock and deadbolt combination. As the door opened, he leaned into the room and announced, "Sonoma County Sheriff. Anyone home?"

There was nothing but dead silence.

Pecou had one hand in his trench coat pocket, the other holding a small penlight flashlight. "You wanna see if those work?" he said, pointing to the wall switches. I flipped them, and we were fully lit up.

Gage's home was in perfect order. There wasn't anything in the kitchen sink or dishwasher. The refrigerator was nearly empty except for some creamer and a cabbage, of all things, sliced in half and beginning to turn brown. There were two small yogurt containers, and a plastic bottle of water. A small wooden table with two chairs was in the center of the room. On two of the walls were pictures of blue water and white sandy beaches advertising travel to the Caribbean. A magazine from a United flight was sitting on the table. Underneath it was an upscale shopping guide for New York, something that could be found in an expensive hotel room.

Pecou drew his weapon and walked alertly through the doorway to what I figured was a bedroom. I flipped through the magazine, looking for dog-eared pages or notes, but found it undisturbed when I heard Pecou.

"Harper. In here."

So now I was Harper. Not froglet, frogman, Godzilla, or the Bane of Yoto.

On the bed was a suitcase nearly full with folded clothes. A pair of non-wrinkle travel pants and a Hawaiian shirt were hanging over the doorway to Gage's bathroom. On the floor was a pair of brown loafers, stuffed with socks that had pink flamingos on them. I got the impression that this was his travel attire for his expected journey to his island.

He'd planned to leave, and something had interrupted him.

CHAPTER 9

My peppy demeanor had evaporated. After seeing evidence of a life interrupted before me, a niggling doubt crept into my psyche. Something was very wrong. I knew he'd been murdered because Pecou had told me so. But seeing that Gage had cleaned his house, locked his door, and left open the suitcase for the completion of his packing told me he wasn't kidnapped or murdered at the cottage.

Pecou was in a pensive mood all the way back to my hotel on the square. He pulled up to the curb and just sat in the car next to me with the motor shut off. Several tourists strolled by, scanning shop windows and trying to look like locals but failing miserably. Someone who lived in Healdsburg wouldn't be checking out every face they passed. They'd be going about their day, used to all the surroundings, including the people.

"I can hear the wheels turning, Watts."

"They are. Notice how Carla didn't ask how John died? That seem funny to you?"

"Like she knew something about it?"

Pecou shrugged. "Maybe. Or had a hunch. Definitely something she's not telling me."

We sat for a few more seconds, watching the parade of tourists pass by. I was getting tired, and a little impatient. "So, what's the plan, Stan?"

"I'm okay with you calling me Watts, but please don't call me Stan."

I didn't bother to ask him why, just complied with his request, feeling a pinch grateful that I didn't have to call him "Detective Pecou" any longer.

"You gonna call Lewis, or stop by at ten o'clock?" I asked.

"I'm going to bring two uniforms with me in case we need to make an arrest. I want that sucker scared shitless so he'll tell me a whole lot more than she did."

"You want me to be there?"

"Only if you want to be. I can always call you tomorrow. I'll be heading back up to the bungalow this afternoon with an evidence team.

"I'll pass on that. I think I should try to locate this trucker, Colgrove."

"You do that. See if you can get an angle for me to question him." He held up the keys. "He's involved, I just don't know how."

"Well, Colgrove is the owner of Gage's pot farm. At least, that's what the deed in my office says."

"Hmmm. So, I'm gonna need copies of those transfers then. Why don't you call me when you have them sent, and then stop by the cottage to see what they came up with. I'm guessing you'll want to see bank statements or anything business-related, right?"

"Yes, there are some holes I need to fill."

"Okay, text me when you're on your way. I'll do the same if I find something earth-shattering. And, Sean—I can call you that now, right?"

"I was getting used to 'froglet.' You can even call me 'asshole' if you'd like."

"What a piece of work you are. At least you don't make it boring. Seriously, Sean, be careful of this guy, Colgrove. If he gets funny on you, just walk away or text me. Make sure he knows I'll be making a call. Find out where he lives, if you can."

"Will do. I think I'm going to use the restroom and then probably just crash, sleep off some of those eggs." I glanced down at my shirtfront. "And change my shirt."

"Good idea."

I made the call to our shared executive assistant in New York, requesting she send an email to my computer with the closing statements and copies of the notes and deeds of trust. I also asked her for a copy of the rental agreement for Miss Bromley and her beau, Lewis.

I removed my shirt and rinsed it in the sink, using a little hand soap, which actually managed to get it clean. But to be sure, I buzzed the front desk and requested that it be laundered, arranging for it to be delivered the next day. This was a service I was used to in New York and was surprised I could get it here.

Next came the call to Colgrove Trucking—the phone number on the key fob Pecou had let me examine. The call went right to voicemail.

"Mr. Colgrove, my name is Sean Harper. I've been tasked with wrapping up Mr. John Gage's affairs. I'm the executor of his estate, out here from New York. I'd like a moment of your time, please, as I noticed several transfers of real estate from Mr. Gage to you recently. I'm only out here for a couple of days, so your cooperation is needed. Thank you, sir." I left my cell number and disconnected.

I toyed with the idea of another shower, feeling that the afternoon would start heating up, or at least more than I was used to. But I just decided to lie down for a nap instead. In a clean white tee shirt and my boxers, I lay on the bed and stared up at the ceiling, hoping to find John's Ariel.

The noise coming from the square, mostly voices but some traffic, was distracting. I found myself in my sleuth mode, trying to make out the words spoken, just like I'd been doing with Ariel in my imagination. I closed my eyes and decided to just relax and fall asleep.

It didn't take long for me to find myself standing in the middle of a familiar jungle, with the same bird and insect noises as before. The thatched hut appeared out of nowhere. This time, the front door was ajar.

I knocked.

The delicate scent of orange blossoms washed my face like a gentle breeze as the door creaked open. Ariel stood, leaning against the doorframe, looking very sad. Her cheeks were moist, and her lip pouted. I knew without asking that she had a broken heart. I wanted to speak to her but remembered what had happened every time I tried in the past.

She shifted to the side and allowed me entrance. Like a surreal movie, several items from my apartment back in New York were there: an antique, spinning globe that my grandfather had given me when I went off to attempt college, a folded flag in its frame from my father's funeral when I was a boy, and my favorite leather reading chair and bookshelf in the corner.

But my eyes soon focused on the sway of Ariel's hips as she walked down a short hallway to a room with tall, floor-to-ceiling sliding doors that opened to the jungle. Another breeze blew in through the screen door and encircled her body, carrying with it the scent of the rich plant foliage. Her long hair was shiny, falling loosely and hanging nearly to her waist. Her graceful arms rose up to adjust the bow at the back of her neck, but when she did so, the one-piece sarong fell in a flutter of silk as if it were a life-sized butterfly.

The fullness of her hips and the indentation of her slim waistline framed the beauty of her perfect ass.

I felt myself inhale sharply, and I awakened, disappointed, sweating and gasping for breath. I gripped my hands together into fists and clenched my teeth. I stared back at the ceiling to see if there was any evidence that what I'd seen had actually been there.

I bolted out of bed, shed my clothes, and turned on the shower. I left the water a little on the cool side. The hotel soap was lemon verbena, a nice compliment to the orange blossom scent still filling my nostrils. Several times during the shower, I turned around quickly because I thought I heard a woman's sigh. I was still searching, listening for unusual sounds as I dried off with the fluffy, off-white towel. After checking the closet, I found a lightweight, waffle-weave robe hanging beside another slightly smaller one and slipped it on.

I lay back on the bed, leaving my robe loosely cinched, then moved my arms so they were outstretched to the sides, and slowly closed my eyes.

Something caught my attention, and I realized I'd been dreaming. I tried to go back to the state I'd been before, hoping to push a few more minutes of sleep my way, but on instinct, I opened my eyes.

She was curled on the bed beside me. Her nude body was tucked under my shoulder, her head resting on the side of my chest. Beneath where her cheek lay, I felt wetness. My fingers searched her face, and I confirmed her tears. I rolled toward her, placing my arms around her waist and shoulder and pulling her to me. She was soft and pliable, as I knew she would be. The scent of the orange blossoms in her hair made my heart thump wildly. I watched her face as I traced the mounds under her eyes with my forefinger, and then followed the touch up with a kiss to each cheek. I kissed her temple, and then down the side of her cheek and along her jaw. In slow nibbles, I traveled to her lips and rubbed mine over hers several times before I claimed her lips.

I felt the arch of her chest, her large breasts pressing against my torso. She'd separated the robe so that we touched each other without the hindrance of clothing.

And then she moaned. Her left thigh rubbed against mine. She pressed her legs together and opened my robe by spreading it with her knees. The cool room was briefly chilling as I felt the moisture from the sweat of my desire. She had slipped beneath me, moving under my body, and her smooth, coffee-colored skin burned from within like a furnace. I wanted her eyes open, so I suckled her left nipple, finishing it off with a mild pinch, and was rewarded with her look of desire that drew me into her world. The trace of a smile appeared as my hand traveled the length of her spine, then down her hip and over the back of her thigh. I bent her knee, bringing it closer to me, and then slipped it over my shoulder. I knew she was watching me kissing toward her core.

As my fingers got lost in the lips of her sex, she covered the backs of my hands with hers, forcing my thumb deep inside her. Her chin rose in the natural arch of a woman in lust. I applied pressure to her throbbing bud and rimmed her opening until I moved in proper position to enter her.

I would have said something, but I didn't want to spoil the moment. I slid her leg off my shoulder, grabbed her hips and pulled her up to my rock-hard cock, then filled her to my hilt, pushing her down and deep into the bed. We continued this rolling motion, delighting in the spring of this new love affair I thought I might die without. Her head whipped back and forth on the pillow as I picked up the pace, clutching at her buttocks and hips, wrapping my arms around her waist and then letting go in a freefall of legs and arms, but still keeping us connected.

She gasped. My seed was coming too soon, but she stilled to feel it, her muscles milking my shaft, extracting everything I had.

I found her ear through the forest of her hair on the pillow. Before I could stop myself, I whispered, "Ariel. I have found you."

All of a sudden, I was alone, humping a large body pillow from the bed, my arms wrapped around its middle. I dropped my hips and straightened my knees, feeling the remnants of my seed spilling onto the sheets. At last came the long satisfying exhale, and the realization that real or fantasy, I could not live without her.

CHAPTER 10

My cell phone rang, and for a few seconds, I was completely disoriented. That used to happen to me back in the killing zones of Afghanistan and Iraq, especially if I'd talked to a buddy or girlfriend back home, and later with Corey and the steamy video calls we used to have when she would do little dress-ups for me. I had to be careful not to let the whole squad see her do it. It was the topic of great conversation around the cave. Some of those poor bastards were still waiting to get laid for the first time and were scared out of their minds, probably thinking about dying without getting any. Yet, as SEALs, we had a reputation for being fearless in the bedroom as well as on the battlefield.

I couldn't remember my dream from earlier, but I knew there was a lot of flesh in it, coffee-colored flesh, and some divine little pink things, too. I remember being fed fresh fruit while we fucked, and I wished I had more details for a second helping.

My first attempt to pick up the phone failed, and I sent it scooting across the carpeting toward the bathroom. I dashed out of bed, still wearing the robe I'd put on just before I fell asleep. The display on the screen said *Colgrove Trucking.*

"Mr. Colgrove?" I barked, out of breath.

A woman's voice answered. "No, Mr. Harper. I'm his wife. Jenny. Barney isn't here right now."

"Sorry to hear that. When will he be around?"

The silence on the other end of the phone had me instantly worried. "I'm not sure." Her voice faded. She fiddled with the phone and then added, "Is there something wrong with all the paperwork, Mr. Harper?"

"No. Not as far as I can tell. I just wanted to go over the last transactions with both of you, if I could."

"So, you've determined that everything was done legally and the property is mine? Ours, I mean."

"Yes. Why would you worry about that?" The hairs on the back of my neck began to stand up like they did when we used to patrol through a quiet, civilian neighborhood, which was usually anything but quiet or purely noncombatant. I sensed something was bothering Mrs. Colgrove, just from the timid sound of her voice. "Is there some problem?"

"No," she said too quickly. "I mean, Barney sometimes takes off on hunting trips, but he always tells me. I never know when he'll be home sometimes, and that's okay. He likes to leave just before the season—um—well, trucking season is anytime, really, but he hauls a lot of gravel and sand for construction. So we're usually busy all summer."

I knew there was something else and she didn't want to tell me. "Could we get together this afternoon, just for a few minutes. I'm trying to wrap up everything and get back to my office in New York as soon as possible."

"I don't know. I'm working this afternoon."

"When do you get off?"

"Not until six. Then I have to pick up the kids at daycare and make dinner. Tonight isn't a good night."

I hated leaving this situation dangling, and I knew that if Detective Pecou were involved, she might be required to take off work. I didn't want to cause her any trouble. For some reason, I wanted to protect her.

"How about a break? Can you take a little time out, perhaps meet me at a coffee shop somewhere we can talk privately?"

"We're nearly done with lunch hour. I came home to check on Barney and got your message. But I've got to get back."

"How about you call in sick, or tell them you had to take some personal time?" I was hoping she'd warm up to me. "Where do you work?"

"Healdsburg Hardware & Nursery. Let me call them and see. I'll call you right back."

"Sure thing."

While I waited for what I hoped would be a yes, I took another shower. At this rate, I'd be scrubbing all the skin off my bones, but I needed to get rid of the remnants of the wet dream.

I dressed and checked my phone for any text messages from Detective Pecou or my office. I received notification of several emails that were sent to my laptop. Before I could open them, Jenny called back.

"Okay, Mr. Harper. They said I could have a few hours off. You want to meet me at the house, or someplace in town? I'd prefer to meet here if possible."

"Perfect." She gave me the address, and I picked up my computer and car keys and headed for my rental car.

It was indeed getting warm, so I put the top down and enjoyed some of the early summer sun. Oddly enough, the windy road to her house took me right past Frog Haven Winery, the bone frog logo on their sign hanging in the breeze at the side of the gravel drive like a reminder of who I had been and who I still was. Row after row of green vines along the country roadway reminded me of a deck of cards being shuffled by some unseen hand. Someone who was way more adept at organizing.

I followed her instructions, turning west as I climbed into some foothills, passing wooded groves, and large, turn-of-the-century homes tucked behind iron gates identified with brass placards. Names like Monteleone, Villa Montalvo and Net Worth Vineyards were snobbishly displayed. This being a Tuesday, most of the wineries were closed.

I was surprised when I came upon the house address next to an old set of stone pillars. I stopped, pushed the intercom button, and was buzzed through, the plain, black metal gate yawning open for me as birds chirped overhead. I traveled as instructed, nearly a mile through several clumps of redwoods, past a small lake, and some vineyards that weren't very well maintained. Weeds grew to the height of the vine's vertical extenders. Some of the leaves had already dried and turned brown from what looked like lack of water or disease.

I passed a large greenhouse on the right, just before the two-story farmhouse in need of paint came into view. Jenny was sitting on the wide steps leading to a wraparound porch. The greenhouse had a red and yellow crest of what I presumed to be their family tree, hanging over its doorway.

I heard the sounds of machinery and noticed it came from the greenhouse. Sides of the translucent plastic walls hissed from the spray of overhead irrigation. I wasn't sure why, but it hadn't occurred to me that this was the property John Gage had owned at one time. I didn't know anything about the greenhouse or pot business, but the long, white structure appeared, unlike the condition of the house or the vineyards, to be of first-class construction. The hip on the roof was nearly as tall as the second story on the farmhouse. The ground around the greenhouse had been weeded and raked to a smooth, manicured condition like at a golf course. Mrs. Cosgrove watched me observing the structure.

"You know John a long time?" she asked, standing and extending her hand.

"Nice to meet you, Jenny. You can call me Sean. No, I wish I'd known him longer. Only about two weeks."

I noted that she didn't ask me how he'd died, or when.

I returned her question with one of my own. "Was he a long-time acquaintance of yours?"

"Barney used to work for John. He put him on the payroll so I could get health insurance. I had cancer three years ago, and we didn't have any coverage."

"Wow. How are you doing?"

"In remission. Fingers crossed." She turned to climb the stairs, and I noted a slight limp on her right side, though she did her best to hide it.

The house was furnished with what I would call Salvation Army chic. It was clean, but nothing matched, and the house seemed only partially filled with furniture.

"You just move in?" I bit my tongue right after I said it, thinking she might take offense.

"That bad, huh? Sorry, we're land poor. And yes, we've only been here about four months. Been working on the..."—she gave me a stern look—"you know about the greenhouses, right?"

"You have more than one?"

"Four."

"Well, I knew what John used to grow, if that's what you're asking."

"This will be our first year. We just finished planting and getting everything set up. Right now, everything we earn goes right back into the business. Hoping it pays off better for us than it did for John."

She handed me a glass of ice water without asking what I wanted. The water tasted delicious, clear and sweet.

I disagreed with her. "John made a lot of money at it, I guess. He had big plans. So, I'd say it turned out quite nicely for him."

"You know about the island, then?"

"I do. He told you about it?"

"Mostly about the girl. He was so excited to move there. It's a shame to work so hard, and just when you're about to enjoy it, you get careless and have an accident. It all goes away in the blink of an eye. I'll bet up in Heaven he wishes he never went surfing that day."

My attention went into high alert. Pecou hadn't mentioned anything about surfing, and I wondered why. On the other hand, from my days of living in San Diego, where surfing was a daily constitution for many of the men on our Team, I knew for a fact that only the most accomplished surfers attempted to work the rocky shores of Northern California. And John didn't look anything like the surfers I knew.

"I didn't know he surfed. But like I said, I only knew him a short time before his death."

"Yeah, I guess he was learning so he could impress his lady in the Caribbean. He was secretly taking lessons. I don't think he told many people. His instructor comes into the store all the time. He told John not to go out on his own, but John was also stubborn, at least that's what Barney told me. If John wanted something, he got it. I can see him ignoring that advice. And it obviously cost him his life."

My head was swimming with questions regarding the investigation and either the lack of information the authorities had, or the fact that they'd acted like I was an ally when I was being played. I wasn't comfortable with either scenario. I wanted to believe I was a good judge of character, and something here didn't match up.

"May I sit?" I asked, pointing to an overstuffed chair with a rip on the right side.

"Sorry, yes. Please." Jenny took the chair perpendicular to mine.

"Jenny, where is Barney?" I decided to be direct.

She stared at her water. "I don't really know. He's been gone four days now." She would clam up if I didn't do something. I could tell she wasn't sure if she could trust me—and I wondered if she was telling me the truth, as well.

"I imagine running this whole enterprise, plus your full-time job and the kids is quite a burden on you. You have any help?"

"Not really. He'll be back. I can make do for a few days. He always comes back. And I have my Smith & Wesson if anything should try and cross me. It's an airweight, and I carry it in my purse all the time."

A shiver went up my spine. "Don't mean to pry, but are you and your husband getting along?"

"I thought we were. But Barney's funny. He keeps secrets." Her eyes suddenly flared with recognition. "Oh! Not like girls or anything, just things he does with his money. Stuff he buys. Equipment. Apparently, he bought another hunting rifle. Tate's gun shop called me to say it was ready for pickup."

"I'm sorry. It must be a lot. No family nearby then to help with the kids?"

"No. Out of state. As you noticed, my evenings are pretty much booked. No time for anything else. We have a good lead worker, and he speaks Spanish, so he runs the crew. Barney could talk with them, but I can't understand a word. I'm fine with that."

"Well, that's good. So, when did he leave again, and when do you realistically expect him back?" I leaned forward and tried to show my concern, which was not an act. I *was* worried about this woman, raising two small children in the middle of a multi-million-dollar pot farm, only armed with an airweight that allowed five shots.

"We got the news about John—what was that, Friday? And the next day, Barney took off. I can't get ahold of him on his cell. He must have gone out of range somewhere."

"Where does he go, usually? Does he visit with anyone? How about his friends?"

"He likes to hunt wild pig up north of Cloverdale, and sometimes, he takes his friends. Lately, he hasn't had any time, we've been so busy."

"Does he stay with anyone?"

"He has a family cabin up there. Nothing is in season, even wild turkey, but I guess Barney didn't care. As far as when he'll be back? Who knows? I'm kinda worried I can't reach him, but it's remote up there. I hope he didn't drive off the road. It would take months before anyone found him."

"What makes you think he's hunting pig?"

"Because he took all his guns, even his handguns. He left me the .38."

A man disappearing with all his guns was doing one of two things. He was going after someone, or he was drawing a predator away from his most valuable possession: Jenny and the kids.

CHAPTER 11

Jenny gave me a brief tour, driving me in a modified golf cart she said they used for transporting tools and equipment between greenhouses. I saw an old four-wheel-drive pickup that must be used for heavy things parked up the hill at Greenhouse #2. The crest that hung over the open doorway was a red dragon over a black shield. The design looked familiar.

Through the doorway, we saw a few farmworkers working over white, five-gallon containers. They were transplanting small seedlings into the plastic bins I assumed they'd spend the rest of their natural lives in. Spanish rock music from a local station blared in the background. Several of the men, and a couple of the women workers looked up briefly, but when they saw Jenny, they went back to their work. Everyone wore white gloves and facemasks.

As we drew to the top of the hill, we came upon the third greenhouse, surrounded by what appeared to be the best of the vineyard, perfectly managed. I'd heard that many vineyards' entire income hinged on a fraction of the total acreage. This was the moneymaking portion. The greenhouse was locked with a chain, but through the Plexiglas, I could see grow lights turned on, and water condensation on the walls.

"How many of these can you fit on this property?"

"We're allowed two more by county ordinance. But we have to save up to get them built. Barney's been working on that."

The view from the gentle rise was outstanding, showing a sweeping vista of the entire Dry Creek Valley. "Does this take a lot of water?"

"Sometimes that's a problem. We have an unusually good ag well here. One of the best on the valley floor."

The crest above the locked door was a grey wolf over a white background. Someone had written *Winter Is Coming* underneath.

"So someone is following the epic saga on TV," I said as I pointed to the plaque I knew to be from the House of Stark.

"That was John. I read the books, so I knew, but Barney—well, he doesn't read much. I had to explain it to him, and he decided to just leave them in place. Thought they might be good luck."

I found that comment odd.

We stopped to admire the famous valley floor and the lushness of all the green rows of award-winning vintages. "You got a little piece of Heaven here, too, I'd say."

"We feel very lucky. John went out of his way for us. We kept saying that it was too good to be true, so when you called, for a bit, I thought perhaps our luck had run out, or maybe I'd been right."

I didn't want to mention that I suspected Barney's luck *had* run out, which would impact her, but since I was a ways from being certain of that conclusion, I kept my mouth shut.

"How did he help you?"

"If you've seen the paperwork, you know he carried paper on this place. Even if our credit was strong and we had tons of money in the bank, we never would have qualified. And in our present situation, with the loans against the truck and the equipment, well, we were just digging ourselves out of a hole after my cancer. So it was truly a miracle."

"I'd say he wanted to leave it to you guys. He must have known you'd work very hard to take care of what he started. He did all these greenhouses, right?"

"He did. Most the surrounding vineyards were in when he bought it. But he's replaced about twenty acres. They don't produce yet. It's always a work in process. Vines have to be upgraded. The greenhouses we man twenty-four seven, and we can harvest two to three times a year, if everything goes right. But the vines are delicate, and of course not climate-controlled. Mother nature can be harsh sometimes."

I was struck with what a hard life it was, even with all the beauty surrounding me.

She walked back to the cart. "You seen enough, or you want to keep going?"

"I need to meet up with someone else this afternoon, so I think we'd best get back."

She drove me back to the ranch house, and I promised to keep her abreast of anything that would affect the farm. I didn't mention John's investigation or that it had been clas-sified a murder, or that a detective would be contacting her next.

"Thanks, and when I hear from Barney, I'll make sure you're the first person he calls."

"You do that. Thanks, Jenny."

As I meandered back down Oak Hill Lane and then back to the main highway headed back to Healdsburg, my instincts told me she'd never see her husband again. I had a sinking suspicion that whatever forces had gone after John could be at play and that they wouldn't take long before they made their move against her. I was struck by how ballsy it was in this day and age to be so obvious.

"You get ahold of Colgrove?" Pecou asked me when he picked up the phone without saying hello.

"That's just it. His wife says he's missing."

I heard a deep sigh into the phone and felt the same way.

"When was the last time she saw him?"

"The day they found out Gage was dead. And there's something else, she thought it was a surfing accident."

"That's what the local TV station said. We didn't think there was any harm in leaving it that way."

"Where'd they get that information?"

"That's not high on my list."

"So, how do you know it was murder? Could they be right? He *was* taking surfing lessons."

"The blunt force trauma doesn't match up, and the coro-ner thinks he was strangled. Perhaps then held under water. We've got skin analysis from under his fingernails coming."

"So, when were you going to tell me all this?"

"Thought it might scare people away. I wanted you to locate Colgrove. If he thought it was a murder investigation, he might not want to be found. And, as far as I know, he could still be our biggest suspect."

"For what purpose? So he can give back the farm John just gave them?"

"Could have been an argument."

"The wife seems like an innocent to me, and very grateful. I don't think she knows anything. And when she finds out—because I didn't tell her—that John Gage's death was murder, she's gonna be scared. Probably won't trust me at all. She's all alone with the wolves surrounding her."

"And we'll be there, too, watching."

I didn't like that Jenny was going to be used as bait. It rose the hackles on my neck and irritated my gut. I had to say something.

"You know, I could be wrong, but I think she's in some danger and has no awareness of it. She lives there with their two kids. She has no family. Barney was her everything. She just thinks he's off hunting. I think part of her knows there's more to it, but she doesn't want to see that right now. You'd better get her some protection."

Pecou ignored me. "Get over here to Gage's bungalow. We'll talk. I got the search warrant for the main house, too. There' s something here at the cottage you need to see."

CHAPTER 12

I was irritated that I couldn't go back to one of my nice dreams. But, it was getting close to dinnertime, and although I'd eaten way too much at breakfast, I was hungry again. My stomach was churning as I drove back to the house on Matheson.

Several other vehicles were present, all marked with Sonoma County logos. Just as Pecou had wanted, a Healdsburg police cruiser was on hand. The two officers stood outside the bungalow, and I caught a quick glimpse of Pecou handing one of them back a cigarette. I looked away before we could make eye contact. I would pretend I hadn't seen that.

The beefy uniforms moved aside as I was introduced and shown into the cottage. I was about to step onto the carpeting when Watts speared me on the chest with his forefinger. "Off. And wear these." He handed me gloves again as he pointed to my shoes. I did as he asked, while he did the same.

"We found some interesting things in the TV," Pecou said.

"*In* the TV?"

"That's what I said."

"That's a helluva place to store things."

"Turns out, it's not a TV, after all." He winked and then continued on through the front door ahead of me.

The television had been turned around and the back removed. Though there was a connection that had been plugged into the wall, the inside of the machine was a storage space. Several boxes of moleskin notebooks were stored in archival-quality containers, each labeled by year.

While I fingered through them, Pecou waited for the other technicians, who were cleaning up, to leave the room.

"So, what do you make of it, Sean?"

"These are records for his pot farm, looks like going back, geez, six years or more." I was astounded.

"Take a look there," demanded Pecou, pointing to the final page on the last ledger from 2011.

I was looking at a staggering number of cash payments in each book, which had started out in 2011, enough to buy an average-sized house in the US, and then rose to figures that could soon purchase half the valley or half the town of Healdsburg. All the numbers were tabulated at the end of the year, and grew until the last cash payment of roughly eleven million dollars just several days before John's death was recorded.

"You notice anything different about this ledger?" Pecou asked.

I looked at the detail with which Gage had written his list of expenses, even breaking down cash payments to workers on the farm, material, and fertilizers, the cost of abatement and trips to the dumps for some of his garbage. He kept a full-on set of books, complete with a balance sheet and profit and loss statement. I couldn't see anything wrong with it. Looking up at Pecou, I shrugged. "Looks about as complete as I've ever seen. He knew how to keep a good set of books. Like he was making sure someone knew exactly how profitable he was. These are the kinds of ledgers you keep when you want to sell your business, especially when it's a cash business. I've seen it with restaurants and such when they take in so much cash. They have no way to verify it, except to make entries like this."

"Nope. That's not it. Think about it, Sean. Where's the money?" he asked, his voice lowered.

I thumbed through the pages, and even searched the archival boxes, sorting through a few receipts that John had saved. Watts was right. There were no bank statements or deposit slips.

"It has to be somewhere," I said. "Have you checked everything?"

"Did he come into your offices with cash or a check?" Watts asked me.

"Cash."

"Then I think that explains it. Only question I have is, where is all the rest of it?"

Evidence samples were labeled, and the crew was sent on their way. They had taken John's suitcases, his shaving kit, and all the toiletry items in the bathroom that he was apparently going to leave behind, plus the clothes he had hanging in the doorway to wear on the plane.

Pecou demanded to keep custody of the ledgers and the six boxes, so they were each placed in large evidence bags and sealed. He took them out to his SUV and placed them in the hatch at the rear.

"Did you search the house in front?" I asked.

"We're gonna wait until we talk to Lewis first. It's the way the order was written, and with as much cash as we're looking for, I'm going to stick to the rules. We're supposed to ask for permission first, and if he refuses, then that goes against him later on. These guys can come back tomorrow."

"So, now we wait. You want to go someplace where we can go over the ledgers?"

Pecou winced. "Shouldn't. I let you see all I could. Don't want to mess with the evidence. I say we go have some dinner and chat a bit. Then we can come back and talk to the two of them."

I was hungry, so when Pecou suggested a good rib joint on the square, I was all for it. I made a complete mess of everything in a one-foot radius. My shirt was smeared with sauce, and I felt black grit lodged between my teeth. I would need my third shower of the day, I surmised.

"Taking you out to eat is like taking a toddler. You sure you fit into that Manhattan lifestyle, man? I just can't see you at those fancy outings with all the rich and famous people." He grinned and showed me that he also had grit between his teeth.

"You forget where I came from, Detective. We weren't the choirboys or the ones with the best manners. I can just about say to the man every one of us on the Teams gave our mothers grey hairs and early graves. My poor mom put up with so much from me, I'm still apologizing for it every time I see her."

He returned a lopsided grin. "Well, that's all right. You turned out okay, I guess. I'm sure she's proud of you now."

"She'd be happier if I'd give her some grandkids."

"Well, that's not for everyone, son. Sometimes, it just isn't meant to be. I seriously hope you have a brother or sister."

It irritated me that he called me "son" when we were near the same age. I decided to let it pass. "I have a little sister. And, yes, I think Mom'll get her grandkids some day."

"Well, there you go. Situation solved."

"You have a family?"

"I'm not a family man, Sean."

"You seem like a decent guy. I can't see why that would be," I prodded. At first, I saw anger on his face, but he took a deep breath and looked at me with slits for eyes.

"Okay, man. You asked for it. You're about to get the whole story, the sad, sorry truth."

I finished off my beer and held up my pint glass. "Looks like I need fortification. You want another?"

"Nah. Not tonight, but you go ahead. You can walk to your room if you get too wasted. And I'm thinking you don't want to do that interview, do you?"

"Not really."

"Okay, then. Shut up and let me tell my story, and then I'll take my leave. You get some good rest, and I'll buzz you in the morning and fill you in, deal?"

"Deal." We shook hands over the carnage of rib bones and barbeque sauce and the occasional half-eaten, beer-battered onion ring. I was beginning to think perhaps Pecou only ate when he was with me, he was so skinny.

"I was enrolled in college back in N'awlins about a dozen years ago. I didn't think I was cut out to go into the military, and I had an uncle who was a Shreveport sheriff, so I thought I could do some work in my favorite city."

"In politics?"

"Nope. Criminal Justice. I knew there were some things my uncle said needed fixin'."

"You're kidding!"

"Hey, a police force is just like any other group of office workers. I'm sure you saw it on your Teams. Some work harder than others. Some, and it's usually only a few, are bad apples. You've seen 'em."

"Unfortunately, yes, I have."

"I was close to graduating, was even going for my Masters when my little sister went missing."

He studied my reaction.

"Fast forward a few frustrating months and then a year and a half of nothing happening with the investigation. I graduated, was now ready for the academy, but I was becoming a regular pest around the force. The FBI were useless. I mean, they said very nice things like they 'had their best people on it.' I could tell just by looking at their faces that they thought she was a runaway. They didn't know my little sister. Pretty, talented. She played the most beautiful piano."

He looked away so I couldn't see that he'd teared up. I found myself holding my breath again. I didn't want to hear the end of the story, but I also couldn't help myself.

"How old was she?" I ventured.

"Sixteen. Smart. Headed for college. Nearly destroyed our family. A family friend told me not to apply for work anywhere near my hometown, that I should move to Florida or Georgia, or maybe go up north. I couldn't go. What if she came back and needed me?"

"How did you get out here?"

"I did get some part-time work, and I also got some security guard work down at the port. That's when I found out about what was going on in N'awlins with the young girls and this jerk with his cult. I talked to a kid down at the docks, who knew my Denise. He told me she'd been shipped out here, to California."

"California? Not Mexico, or—"

"No. California. They got a lot going down in Mexico too, but this little group runs out of Cali. Turns out, for a time, she was right here in Healdsburg. I nearly found her."

"Here?"

"Yessir. As crazy as that sounds. I came out and worked all the leads we had, me and a buddy from school who was more than a little sweet on her. We got close. Very close."

"But you never found her? What do you think happened to her, if I can ask?"

"I just know she's alive. Don't know where. But I decided I wasn't going to leave here until I found her, one way or the other. But, Sean, I know she's not dead. I can feel her presence. Does that sound strange?"

Having been fucking a dream every night recently, I didn't find it strange at all.

"Hell no, Watts. I believe in those sorts of things. And evil exists all around us. You probably know about that better than I do. But nothing is really as it seems. People are so dumb, vulnerable."

"See, we have that in common, you and I. We both hate to see innocent people hurt. I'm telling you now, as much as I think I'm doing good work as a public servant, if I catch the man who put a hand on my Denise, I'd take the satisfaction of putting him out of his miserable life. I scare myself sometimes."

"You have a brother here. Over there, you do your best, but at the end of the day, all you can do is rely on your brothers. Without them, we'd never get out alive. You can't trust anyone else. They can be compromised, they misunderstand, or start believing some of the horseshit they've been fed over the years."

Watts picked up my thought and ran with it. "And over here, they get tainted by greed or the same sort of horseshit you see on TV every day. There are some days when I don't recognize my own country, my own people."

I knew this man wouldn't stop until he found his sister, and that some day, he would. "What about your buddy, and your mom?"

"Mom passed. Died of a broken heart, so that's on them, too. She was never very healthy anyway, but losing Denise just took the life right out of her. My buddy went home for a wedding and met some little thing and...oh, boy, they got three babies already. Priorities change. I went to the academy out here and they let me do my thing at the Sonoma County Sheriff's Department. And that suits me fine. And I wait to see my sister again some day, and some day I will."

There are some men who never give up. I could see that Watts and I were the same.

"So, is the search over, then?"

"Officially? Probably. Stone-cold. Am I finished? No way."

I sipped my beer. I was tired from all the sleep I wasn't getting because of the dreams and the rich food I'd been consuming in greater quantities than I was used to. And my workouts were interrupted. But I wanted to be his backup. I didn't want this man going into the interview alone.

"Look, maybe I can come along and—"

"No, son. You go back to your hotel and get a good one. I never get to bed before midnight anyway. I watch all the reruns of *NYPD Blue* and *CSI*. They get so much wrong, it's entertainment."

If I had more energy, I'd have sparred with him about using that term "son" again. Then I remembered what I'd wanted to remind him of. "One other thing, Watts. We have to protect Jenny Colgrove. I think Barney has been tampered with, and she's not going to have anyone to protect her if he's out of the picture. She's sitting on a gold mine. Here we are, looking for millions in cash. She's sitting on the goose that lays the golden egg. One little woman with two small kids, armed with a handgun, and it isn't a man-stopper."

"I get you. I can see to it she gets in touch with those attorneys I told you about. So, what makes you think something's wrong, other than the fact that he's missing? You said he liked to hunt?"

"Watts, he ordered another rifle from a local gun shop, but he never picked it up before he left. And he brought all his guns with him on that trip, if it was one. He didn't say good-bye to her or tell her when he'd be back. Even took his handguns. Does that sound like someone casually hunting wild pigs?"

CHAPTER 13

I hesitated to leave Watts, but he got the call he'd been waiting on. Lewis was back home. The detective called for the uniforms to meet him over at the house.

I slapped his hand when he tried to pick up the bill, giving him a scowl resembling the roaring flame growing inside my belly. I knew I'd be up all night, and then the next day—well, I knew it would be painful. But damn, it was worth it. I made a resolution to myself that this would end. I decided my morning routine would be resumed. I'd go for a run and find a gym open early.

Strolling through Healdsburg Square, I was struck by how normal everything seemed. It was a weekday, and everything was winding down. The evening was warm, and people were filling up trendy restaurants. Tourists were window-shopping in now-closed stores. I paused in front of a local bookstore and made a note to visit it tomorrow if I had time.

This would have been a nice evening to walk with some-one hand-in-hand, and if I were honest, I was feeling a little blue. Maybe it was the alcohol talking, but I was fed and had a nice buzz from the beers, yet I was not in any way satisfied with how the day had gone, or even how my trip had gone so far. At every turn, there were more questions.

A couple of young ladies walked down the sidewalk together and gave me a look I might have returned in my younger years. I knew where all that led. Heck, with Corey, I'd had some of the best of all that excitement, and I had done it in style. Was it my brothers in arms I missed? The action? Danger and exploded relationships seemed to follow me like a dark cloud. I was a man of action with nothing to do.

Detective Pecou had his own host of issues from his past. Poor Jenny Colgrove was certainly headed into a black hole, I was sure. But tonight seemed like the quiet before the storm. During deployments, these were the evenings when you cleaned your equipment, took apart your sidearm ten times and then oiled and cleaned it. If it was a jump, you packed and re-packed your chute. Stitched anything that had torn, adjusted a pocket or patch so things could be retrieved quickly in one motion. I might have played a game of cards or a video game. Or watched a porn video in one of the rooms the bachelors had, along with their substantial stash of maga-zines. That had been my job as a newbie frog, to carry the all-valuable good ol' US porn for the morale of the troops. I laughed when I recalled the LPO telling me I was no longer a newbie, and them giving the job to a nice virgin, Christian boy just to rub it in.

I turned around, thinking perhaps someone was following me, and saw the two girls sashaying down the sidewalk, snuggling and giggling to themselves. I wasn't a person of interest to anyone, and yet I felt like a target just the same.

Tomorrow, I'd have to go to a copy store and get the information on my computer printed for Pecou. I couldn't check in with my boss in New York because it was too late. I should have done that earlier today, but it had never occurred to me. I opted for a message I knew he'd get in the morning.

"Hey, Sal. This is Sean. I'm working with the detective who visited us last week. I've looked at the properties in the transfer, and we're trying to find things related to my client's assets. So far, I haven't found much. I'm attempting to wrap this up because everything is now a police matter, so there's little I can do. Hoping to get home by Friday at the latest, but it won't be sooner, I don't think. Give thanks to your gal for getting me the deeds, which I have to turn over to the detective." I hesitated but figured I'd just be honest with the man who had agreed to cover my desk for a few days. "Never done this kind of thing before, so if you have any suggestions, I'm all ears. I'll be checking in with Roger Sampson. Anything new, I'll let you know. Have a good one."

I got Roger on the next call. The sound of dance music in the background made interference.

"Hold on a minute, Sean. I'm walking outside," he said.

The background grew quiet, but I still heard a drum beat that told me he was clubbing and that the night was still young for him.

"Okay, that better?"

"Much. So, I just wanted to let you know what was going on here. You have any idea where Gage banked? I can't find a record of where he kept his money, and he had a lot of it to keep track of."

"I hear you. I will check on that in the morning—"

"Which will be about right my time, since you won't get in until noon."

"Shut the fuck up, Sean. You do remember what he did, and from the information we discussed, he did a lot of it in cash."

"That's what I'm finding. But did he have a banking relationship here? A checking account somewhere? You get any recent bills?"

"Nope. I never have. Might be they're still coming, but I haven't seen a thing. Besides, I thought he said everything was coming to your office."

"So what does an executor do in a case like this? I mean, he could have opened a safe deposit box anywhere in town, or in half a dozen places nearby. Or even someplace between New York and California, for that matter."

"You do the best you can. Legal notice going in the paper, and I've arranged one for the *Herald Recorder* there. All the local attorney firms will see it, most of the banks, too. I think the publication should be out sometime this week."

"Okay."

"You need to get me the death certificate showing the cause of death, too. I need that before we can disburse anything other than the trust fund you're using now."

"We have one, but cause of death is still labeled pending."

"That's not going to fly. How long before you get something definitive?"

"Pecou knows we need it. I'm to check in today. Did you look over the property transfer deed? Does anything look fishy to you?"

"Why? You mean his ranch sales?"

"Yes."

"Not that I noticed. Is there some problem?"

"The husband of the couple Gage sold the property to has gone missing. Hoping this isn't another unfortunate event here. If he's gone, there will be difficulty with the wife paying the note payments in the future. I know there was a deferral, but that will be up in six months."

"I hear you. Well, let's hope that's not the case. God, I'd hate to foreclose on a woman who just lost her husband."

"You know it happens in the real world. How many times did we hear that? Someone bites it overseas, and then we get home and the wife and kids have lost the house."

"Bloodsuckers."

"Amen, brother. Let's just pray it isn't that scenario."

"But your gut says otherwise, right?"

"Yup. You know the feeling. I just get"—I waited for a couple to walk past me before I continued—"chills walking around here like something big is going to blow up. It's too damned normal and quiet."

"Effects of war, my brother. I think you have an overactive imagination. You need to get laid. Too bad Corey is out here."

"That's not the solution, and you know it." It still pissed me off when Roger reminded me how she'd looked on those videos she sent me when we were overseas.

"Suit yourself. So, bro, I'll catch you later, okay? Best of luck, and seriously, dude, compared to where we've been, you think Northern California is dangerous? I think most the people on the planet would consider you a nut job. Chill. And if you can't chill, then get drunk and go to bed."

He was right, of course. I put my phone back in my pocket and headed back to the hotel. Once back in my room, I checked my messages, and then shut it down. I stripped and took a nice, leisurely shower. It felt good to get the barbeque beard off my face. I put on the robe I'd learned to enjoy, even dabbed a bit of aftershave on my cheeks and combed my hair after I brushed my teeth.

What the fuck are you doing?

Staring at myself in the mirror, I didn't look like a nut job, but I sure felt like one. I was about to have an encounter with an invisible girl on an island I'd never visited. As much as I doubted my sanity, there was a part of me that knew I'd see her again tonight. I might be dreaming, but it was as real as it ever could be.

I gave myself the James Bond 007 shot to the face, winked at myself, and headed to the bedroom. I was a prick, all right.

I slipped under the covers, leaving the robe untied in front. Stretched out on my back, I closed my eyes and did some deep yoga breathing, allowing the sleep to creep up on me.

It didn't take long before I heard the waves pounding on a beach. I knew that beach as if I'd walked it dozens of times. I heard the same sea birds calling. There was a steel drum playing in the distance. I was lying under the shade of a tree with large fronds. My fingers felt for warm sand and found a thin flannel covering, warmed by the sun. I squeezed the material into my fist, and before I could let go, I felt a warm hand take mine, unpeel my fingers, and place them on the side of her face.

I knew who it was. She smoothed my hand around under her ear. I gently pinched her lobe and then allowed her to move my fingers across the front of her face where my thumb brushed against her full lips as she smiled. I remained with my eyes closed and smiled in return.

I heard the tinkling of the silver charms from the bracelet on her delicate wrist as she drew my hand down the front of her chest, stopping just before I could feel the mounds of flesh begin to rise. My fingers chronicled her heavy breathing. Her other hand was doing something, and as I heard the rustle of fabric, I realized she'd pulled her shirt down to her waist, and my palms were filled to overflowing with her warm breasts. I had to see this.

She was sitting in a pile of skirts, her knees bent, protruding from the mound. Her white blouse hung at her waist. And my right hand explored the wonder of her chest, first one side and then the other. Her eyes followed me as I propped myself up, leaned forward, and suckled her breast. Then, both my hands felt the glory of her warm, smooth body as our lips came slowly together and touched. The kiss went right to my groin. She let my palms wander as our tongues explored. I devoured her inhale when my fingers walked the delicate plank of her left thigh to discover her core at the junction of her thighs.

With the water still pounding on the beach and the resulting hissing sound of its retreat, I lifted her skirt and ducked beneath them. She rose to her knees as my hot tongue found her nether lips, and I tasted her for the first time.

Her hands massaged the tops of my shoulders as she whispered words to me. My appetite was not even partially satisfied, as my cock sprang loose, no longer pressed down by the sheets of my bed. Her hand found me and squeezed as I lapped her juices and sucked for more.

My thumbs pushed back her lips. My teeth scored over her bud, and I enjoyed her shiver before she responded with another squeeze. Her fingers found my balls and pulled back and away, then returned to give me a squeeze from my root to tip. I left my thumb pressed against her bud and brought my head from under her skirts to lead her to straddle me.

I remained pressed against her as she rode me in gentle motions, her fingers puling on her breasts, her wrist jewelry glistening in the afternoon sun, her dark hair falling over her shoulders and one long strand across her chest. I lifted her skirts to see the place of our union, how her bare sex traveled up and down my shaft.

I could have spent all night with this island girl, lovingly giving me the only thing I needed this evening. Her face bore the expression of the orgasm I felt through her shudders. She bit her lip and pushed down firmly against me, sending me deeper as she exploded into a million pieces.

It was natural, this mating, like I'd known her my whole life. The sounds of her voice were muted and I so desperately wanted to hear her, or have her whisper something I understood in my ear. Her moans echoed along the beach. The tropical breeze flew through her hair and kissed her shiny cheeks until I realized she was crying again.

I frowned, concerned that perhaps I'd hurt her, but she arched back one more time and then pressed herself against my hips before she collapsed against my chest. Her gentle shaking as she sobbed broke my heart. I suddenly felt like I'd taken something that wasn't mine to have. Was John still alive out there in the border of the jungle, watching us mingling before him? I turned my head to look but saw no one. The jungle loomed darkly and revealed nothing but petals of lush green, bobbing in the wind.

I sifted my fingers through her hair, rubbing her scalp. I kissed the side of her face. I didn't want to whisper anything to her, but my lips touched her ear. I let her feel my warm breath and the pumping of my heart, so desperate to speak to her. Her arms were around my torso, and at last, she rose, her forearms against my shoulders as she looked at me. I let my palms travel up from the backs of her thighs and over her buttocks, along the valley of her waist and then up to rest on her shoulders. First with one side and then the other, I brushed her cheeks with the backs of my fingers on my right hand.

I knew what it would mean, but I couldn't help myself. I said it again to her, "Ariel, I have found you."

And, of course, she was gone before I'd finished my last word.

My chest was still sweaty and warm from where her body had lain across mine, my heart pumping wildly and my breathing still hard. My right hand was in the air above my chest, so I let it drop softly to the bed.

She had been there. I had loved her on that beach. In my mind, I saw it all, the blue water, the white surf, and the sounds of the waves. As I stared at the shadows falling across the white ceiling of my hotel room, the outside night noises filled the space.

And with them, the faint scent of orange blossoms.

CHAPTER 14

My morning run was just what I needed. I took a left on Matheson Street and ran past the neighborhood with John Gage's house still looking the same as it had yesterday, past the school, and then followed the road as it dropped down into yet another valley below, peppered with little farms.

It was barely seventy degrees, perfect weather for a run. Traffic was light. I couldn't imagine a nicer day to be outside. I decided to continue running, taking a detour through another older neighborhood adjacent to the Matheson one, then up and down some slopes and back around to another main drag into town. That's when I noticed cars with children being shuttled off to school and signs that some of the bakeries and coffee shops were open, other stores beginning to set out their wares.

I checked my pulse and my steps and was pleased by both readouts. Though starved, which now seemed to be my continual state of being, I decided to go for a juice smoothie instead of a big breakfast.

I stretched in the square, finding several other runners using the same park benches and lampposts to do the same thing. We waved at each other, and I headed for the juice bar I'd passed along the way.

The younger crowd was lively, mostly high school kids on their way to classes. Occasionally, someone in a suit came by and picked up wheatgrass shots in a to-go container for the office crew.

I got a healthy blueberry and kale blended smoothie with extra protein and downed it in about thirty seconds, tossing the cup. I jogged toward the hotel entrance for my shower. Along the way, I got a call from Sal, so I slowed down to a walk to take it.

"You ready to move out there and open up an office for me?" he asked.

"God, it's nice here. Imagine being able to afford to live here and choosing to move? Gage must have been nuts." I knew it was a lie, but the healthy banter with my boss was what was called for.

"So, you mentioned you're having a hard time finding things for Gage?"

"We used to hear about these guys. Now, I know it to be true. Apparently, he ran an all-cash business, off the grid. I can't imagine what he planned to do with his taxes when he reported the sale of the property this year, and the dividends from the account he had with us. I don't know what in the hell he was thinking."

"Maybe he never intended to report any of that."

"It's looking that way, Sal. Do people really do that, just disappear and go off the grid?"

"Just rumor. Everyone I've heard about has gotten caught and damned near lost it all trying to evade the Feds. So, do they have the cause of death yet? You can't do anything without that."

"Roger told me. I'll be checking in with Detective Pecou first thing here. He's been as cooperative as he can be. But, short of walking the entire town, asking each bank if they had an account with John Gage, there's not much else to do but find his killer. I'm still thinking there's a safe deposit box somewhere or a bank account we haven't found yet. We'll find it."

"Well, stay as long as you need. Everything here is good." He asked me about a minor client issue, and I helped him out with some suggestions, and we agreed to talk again when I had news or was coming home.

I dialed Detective Pecou next.

"Everything okay? You sound out of breath."

"I went out for a run this morning. Had myself a juice, and even checked with my office. They said to remind you that they still need a completed death certificate."

"No kidding. I'm hoping by tomorrow. Could be today. I was told last night we can officially rule it murder. It wasn't a surfing accident."

"That's going to be a shock to Jenny Colgrove. So, how did the interview go last night?"

"I think Lewis had something to do with it. But he wants to blame this Colgrove guy. Said at one time they'd been thick as thieves. He thought maybe they'd had a falling out."

"So you didn't bring Lewis in?"

"He was cooperative. I didn't need the uniforms, just protocol, and he didn't look very nervous either. Only motive is the cash. But since we have no evidence of it, it would be pretty hard to charge him."

"We got the ledgers."

"And the first thing a defense attorney is going to do is ask for evidence of theft. How are we going to prove that?"

"So that means you're ready to go talk to Jenny Colgrove."

"I think she's next. I won't hear anything from the evidence team until later this afternoon—unless something interesting turns up."

"You got her number, then, or should we go by her work?"

"I say we meet her at work. It wouldn't be unlikely for someone to question her about the whereabouts of her husband."

Jenny was nervous this morning, especially when Pecou told her that Gage's death had been ruled a murder. She gave us the address of the hunting cabin in Cloverdale and confirmed that she still hadn't heard from her husband. She didn't hide her concern this time, even in Pecou's presence.

She looked to me. "Do you think I'm in danger?"

I thought it was curious that she asked me and not the detective.

"Jenny, is your operation self-sustaining? I mean, does your foreman have everything he needs if you were no longer there?"

"But it's our home."

"I understand that. But if Barney is gone, if you were my wife, I'd ask to have a relative come stay with you. Or, have you move there." I looked at Watts. "She could do that, couldn't she?"

I could see he wasn't pleased with the suggestion.

"Let's find your husband first," he barked back, his arms crossed. "I think we may be going off half-cocked. Let's not assume the two events are related. But we do need to talk to your husband about some things."

"Okay. We have payday coming up. After that, I'm not tied here unless the foreman needs something." She rolled her eyes. "Though he always needs something."

"You pay by check or cash?" I suddenly thought of something I hadn't considered before.

"Check."

"You bank in town?"

"Sure. John and Barney had a joint account downtown. We just kept it open afterwards and use that. John signed off on it."

"You deposit much in there?" Pecou saw my line of questioning.

"We get paid by the dispensaries every quarter. John left some operating capital there, but we get our first decent payment August first. We sell organic seedlings to some of the stores who are licensed to sell to card-carrying members for their own use."

"Later, you get paid after the harvest?" Pecou asked.

"That's right. Around Christmas."

"So, how much are you carrying in there now?"

"My payroll is usually about fourteen thousand a month. We have nearly fifty thousand in the account. But we'll use all that up right about the time we get our money from the dispensaries. That's what they're doing right now, transplanting seedlings, mostly for us, but some for the resale trade."

"Anyone else have access to the money in that account?" Pecou persisted.

She shook her head. "Just Barney. And me, of course. John's name is still on the account, but he can't withdraw money anymore. He set all that up before he left the last time."

"What bank do you use?" I asked.

"First National of Healdsburg. Just near the square."

"Did John have any accounts there since he used to bank with them?"

"No. He said everything was closed. He mentioned that to me himself. All he had was a safe deposit box for valuables, you know."

Pecou and I shared a gaze, and I knew where we were headed next.

The bank manager was helpful, especially since I had the papers from Roger giving me authority to collect any items that belonged to John. Pecou produced the current certificate of death with the cause still listed as "pending."

He made a phone call and had a local locksmith come to drill out the lock. I promised him the estate would reimburse him for the cost of doing so. Our outlook was hopeful since it wasn't a tiny box but one of the larger ones that could hold a considerable amount of money.

After the locksmith had finished, the manager hovered around the table, curious as to what was inside. Pecou turned to him, and without saying a word, the manager left.

I flipped open the lid and was disappointed to see that the box was nearly empty. At the bottom was a large, folded up and yellowed piece of paper.

Pecou put on his gloves and unfolded the paper on the table next to us, and I knew right away what it was. It was the original map, the one that had been reduced and photocopied, the one that Roger had sent to me with the deeds and closing statements. On the original, the lines separating the four quadrants were easier to read and appeared to follow the natural terrain of the island. I noted the initials I couldn't read on the smaller map.

They weren't initials at all, but crests, or symbols. I looked at the designs and realized where I'd seen them before. Each of the four quadrants was labeled with an insignia, just like the signs on the outsides of the greenhouses at John's old ranch. Even the one labeled,

Stark
Winter Is Coming.

CHAPTER 15

We put the map in another evidence bag and sealed it, placing it in Pecou's SUV. I hopped in, and we raced up to Cloverdale with Jenny's directions.

I told Pecou about the symbols on the greenhouses.

"Why would he label them like that? I don't see the point. Like he has four worlds there? You think that's it?" he asked.

"I think that's where the money is."

"Seriously?"

"My guess is he was going back and forth, bringing cash to the island. The last one he brought to me, and then he was going to be gone. He'd sold his property, and he was outta here. Wonder what kept him?"

"Something important enough that he mailed that package to you, Sean."

"I think he did that because he was heading out of the country."

"I'd bet anything he did it because he was scared of what he found here. I think it was the last voluntary thing he did. I think we need to take a closer look at it."

"It's back in my office under lock and key. And I opened it up before I knew who it was from. Without gloves."

Pecou rolled his eyes.

"I didn't know," I said as I shrugged. "Just brochures, copies of things you already have, but I'll take a second look, and let you know."

"Appreciate that."

The freeway was a straight shot north. The scenery was beautiful, a continuation of the brown and green hills all over Healdsburg. Cloverdale was about ten degrees hotter, and with a population of fewer than ten thousand, it was only a bit smaller than Healdsburg, but just a little far from the San Francisco crowd, so it didn't have the wineries and tourism business, which meant the restaurants were sparse. But for a main town USA, it could pass for something I'd seen in the Midwest, except for the golden hills looming on nearly all four sides.

North of town was a winding road thought to be an old stagecoach line. Although it was paved, it wasn't much wider than a single lane road with shoulders, so Pecou had to go very slowly. Locals didn't, though. We had some close calls. My hands were sweating when we reached a crossroads, and I indicated that we needed to go left.

After fifty feet, there was no pavement at all. It wouldn't be very passable in the wintertime, but this time of year, it was dusty, yet relatively easy to navigate. Huge oak trees with some redwoods mixed in created a dark green canopy that was refreshing in the afternoon air. Pecou slowed down and lowered his window, looking out at the forest surrounding us. I lowered my window as well and remarked on the beauty of the place.

My phone clunked, indicating a message or change in service, and so did Pecou's. Checking the reception, I told him, "We're out of cell coverage here. That's what Jenny said about this place. We must be getting close."

After making a wrong turn, we veered off down a rutted dirt road heavy with weeds and brush. Branches slapped the sides of the car, so I closed my window. As we turned the corner, a dirty red pickup truck was parked facing out, next to a tiny house made of peeler logs. A fire pit was in the front yard, set up for roasting a large animal over coals. Nothing remained on the spit. A large black kettle sat on flat stones to the side.

Pecou unsnapped his holster and switched off his safety, and I suddenly felt bare, not having brought anything to defend myself with. Pecou leaned over and drew a snub nose .38 from his glove box. "I know you know how to use this. Use it only for your protection, or mine. You keep this out of site."

"Rogert that, sir."

I tucked it in the back of my pants and let my shirt hang over my waistband.

Pecou walked with his piece extended in front of him. "Sonoma County Sheriff. Anyone home?"

We waited for a sound that would never come. A large black bird flapped its wings unexpectedly, scaring us both, but we soon shifted our focus back to the front door. In a normal situation, I'd have offered to go around the back, but there was no way anyone inside would miss the fact that we drove up together in the front seat.

Pecou announced us again, and there was still no answer.

I scanned the forest, looking for any movement, some flash of bright color, or shiny object, some sound of a branch being stepped on or a rock crumbling underfoot. But everything was peaceful, and in any other setting, I would have considered it beautiful and serene.

We were at the windowed front door of the cabin, which had been built right on the ground without a slab or foundation of any kind, and although it had been repaired throughout the years, it still looked very rough. I couldn't see Jenny or her kids spending any time up here. I wondered about running water and power. A large blue propane tank on the right side answered that question.

The detective knocked loudly. "Sonoma County Sheriff's Department. Anyone home?"

He protected the glare with his palm on the window and peered in. All of the sudden, he stuck his Glock back into his holster and swore, then turned the handle and nearly tore the door off its hinges.

I followed behind him, suddenly needing what Pecou had already retrieved for himself—a handkerchief. The stench was nearly eye-watering. A man in a red plaid work shirt and blue jeans had been sitting in a spindle-backed chair but was now slumped to the side and lying on the dusty wooden floor. His brains had been blown out with something big like the high-powered hunting rifle lying by his side. It wasn't an impossible shot, but something that would have taken some coordination to do since the impact was the back of his head.

His brains and most of his teeth and the rest of his face were scattered all over the ground at our feet.

I was using my shirt to cover my nose. "I'm guessing this is Barney," I said through the fabric. I nearly retched.

Watts didn't answer, walked carefully over to the body, and touched the man's right hand, which had contorted in on itself in a death grip reflex I'd seen many times. The fingers were completely stiff. The blood was deep burgundy and soaked into the man's shirt, and looked like red fiberglass material in pools here and there, dotted with purplish-brown chunks of brain matter. Even if I knew what Barney looked like, I'd not be able to identify him now.

While Watts examined the body with his penlight, I asked for an evidence bag. With my pocketknife, I scraped a bit of the dried blood up and flaked it into the bag and closed it. In the field, we generally liked to bring back a whole finger or a toe for a DNA match, but I figured this would suffice. I handed the envelope back to the detective.

I dropped my shirt since the room had begun to air out with the front door open. Pecou had reached into Barney's jeans pocket and retrieved his wallet.

"Says he's Barney Colgrove. But I wouldn't be able to match the picture." He shrugged and went back to examining contents of the wallet.

"You need anything else?"

"Don't touch anything, but can you snap some photos?" He handed me his cell phone.

"Sure. Here, you hold out the license, and I'll snap that, too." Pecou did so, and I took pictures of the social security card and driver's license spread out between his palms.

"Be sure to get the bottoms of his boots, and I want pictures of the hands."

I circled and took nearly fifty shots and asked if he wanted to review them, which he declined.

The cabin was sparsely attired. An opened ammo box was in the bedroom at the rear of the little place, rounds splayed out over the unmade bed and one on the floor. Barney's backpack was unzipped, and another pack, probably the one containing his guns, had fallen beside the bed. Judging from the weight of the bag, I assumed everything was still there.

I knew Pecou was piecing things together as best he could while searching for something to focus on. Carefully pulling back curtains, he glanced outside several times. I didn't bother his thoughts.

"Make sure you get this," he said, aiming at the mess on the bed. I did so.

"I'm going out back to look around."

"Knock yourself out, but don't touch the truck or anything in the vehicle, okay?"

Next to the red pickup were a couple of tracks from a two-wheeled vehicle. Then I saw a different tire pattern, so I took pictures of both of them. I saw Barney's footprints, but I also saw several other pairs of tracks, and one, in particular, had compressed the earth over Barney's print. I thought it was odd that the truck had been turned around to head out before parking it, and it underscored the fact that Barney was trying to give himself every opportunity to get out of Dodge quickly if he needed to.

"You find anything?" Pecou asked me as he joined me outside.

"Looks like two sets of bikes, see here and here?"

Pecou nodded.

"I took the pictures. And I also shot this." I showed him the footprint that would match Barney's work boots, with the newer tread on top of it. "These could have been from before, but Barney's print looks pretty fresh, as does the other one."

"Good catch. Okay, I say we leave everything but this, the rest of his stash and the rounds." He held up the rifle, wrapped in two pillowcases, and the black bag, which he handed off to me. I placed them in the back of his SUV.

"That it?"

"I couldn't find anything else in the house. And it didn't look like he had company. He brought enough junk food to last him a week, though."

Our parting gift to the scene was to stretch some yellow and black crime scene tape across the front of the cottage and tie in bushes at the sides. The door was closed, and Watts said he'd checked the windows.

"Pity the sonofabitch who has to open that door next, though. These temperatures can get pretty extreme up here during the daytime."

"Roger that. Glad I won't be here." I handed him back the cell phone.

We headed back the same way we'd come. When at last we had service, Pecou called his office and ordered the coroner and his team to come up to the property.

And then I got a call from Roger.

"Hey, Roger. I'm in a spotty area. Not sure the reception is good enough."

"No problem, if you cut out, I'll wait for you to call me back."

"Fair enough. What did you find out?"

"Not much. Afraid I struck out here as far as banking. Only thing I get at the office is rent checks, but it's not the first, so I haven't gotten any yet. On his schedule of assets form, he doesn't list any cash anywhere, nor does he list any items in a safe deposit box. Didn't list any jewelry, furniture. Nothing except for household things he donated to the women's shelter."

"So, all he owns is the island and the house in Healdsburg, then?"

"Oh, he has assets. The two million blanket loan on the ranch is an asset. So is the trust fund here for maintenance and administration. And, of course, the money in your portfolio account. All that's sizeable comes up to about twelve million eight hundred thousand and some change. Plus the value of the island, which he pegged at about four million. So that's about sixteen million eight hundred sixty-three thousand, give or take a few hundred thousand."

I whistled and felt Pecou's eyes on me.

"Anything look funny about the transfer?" I barely got the words out, the car was bouncing so much. We finally came to paved road, and I breathed a sigh of relief.

"Nope. Barney Colgrove and his wife hold the property as joint tenants, their shares being equal. If something's gone south with the husband—"

"Roger, we just found him dead."

"Oh, Christ. What a mess. Does the detective think it's related?"

"How could it not be?"

"So we got two bodies now. You just make sure you don't become number three, okay?"

"I promise."

"Well, Jenny will inherit everything automatically, unless they don't have a will. Then the property has to be evaluated and, depending on the value, it might have to go through probate. She wouldn't like that one."

"And to find the girl, to inform her, we have an address?"

"A trust company in Antigua. She'll have to file a claim and record the property in her name. I'm looking for an attorney firm you can use when you go there."

The thought of stepping on the white sandy beach I'd been dreaming about gave me pause. My pulse quickened.

"Sean, you still there?"

"I'm here."

"You finish up there as best you can, get the process going on selling the house, and then let's get you to Antigua for your real adventure."

CHAPTER 16

I accompanied Pecou over to the hardware store where we told Jenny about her husband. She nearly collapsed in my arms. It was obvious that her grief over losing Barney wasn't as strong as the fear of her unknown future without him. And I could see she was wondering about her children's safety, as well.

Her manager was kind enough to give her the rest of the day off, again. Several of her co-workers offered to help her with meals and picking up the kids, but she neatly refused them all.

She would have a lot of arrangements to make, and luckily, I knew she had enough money to pay for some of those expenses. Her stiff constitution kept the tears from appearing on her face, but I was certain she'd collapse when she was finally alone. I gave her my card and told her to call if she needed anything in the next couple of days, and even after that if required. And, I told her to use a good local attorney for all the upcoming paperwork and filings that were sure to come. She said she already had one.

The detective promised to give whatever support she might need, and even offered to have a guard posted at her home in the evenings, but again, she turned him down.

Pecou would be working with the forensics team and the coroner, so I was on my own again, and glad of it. I informed Sal of our sad findings from the day and alerted him of my need to get to Antigua soon. We tossed around some dates, and he said he'd have his assistant check on travel details.

After the call, I wished I had the envelope John had sent me, which I'd left back in New York. Now that Colgrove had also been murdered, I wanted to look over the information my client had thought to send me at the last minute. I was sure there was something there I'd overlooked or something that would help me find Miss Ariel. Just the thought of her name brought a prickly feeling to the back of my neck.

Next, I called Zak and brought him up to date with everything.

"You remember Nick Dunn from back when you were with the Teams?" he asked.

"I think so. Blond kid. Pretty full of himself?"

Zak laughed. "Weren't we all? Well, his wife has her real estate license up here if you're thinking of putting the house on the market."

"As a matter of fact, yes, I was going to set that up. But I'm dancing around a double murder investigation, so not sure if they're done with the property."

"I'll have her give you a call, and you can explain it to her. You'll like Devon. They have a winery down in Bennett

Valley. Not sure if you ever came up on those R&R's they used to do before Nick got married. His sister ran a nursery there."

"No. I think I'd have remembered that. And Nick was an arrogant prick, unmarried."

"That was Nick. He scared me to death when I was just coming on. Now, with two kids and a winery to run, he's fairly domesticated. He got injured during one of the ops, just like I did. They medically discharged him."

When Devon called, I offered to meet her over at the winery, instead of making her haul the kids up to Healdsburg to meet me. The drive down the freeway was pleasant, although packed with more traffic than up north. I still couldn't complain since owning a car in New York was problematic. The city was easy to get around in once you learned how to use public transit.

Turning off the freeway, the two-lane country road was more to my liking, as it meandered past more vineyards and little ranchettes. As instructed, I turned at the lavender-colored sign that read, *Sophie's Choice Winery*, and drove the short distance through fields of lavender, bordered by hedge roses and an explosion of bright flowers. The showroom and visitor center was adjacent to a large hall. Zak told me it was a popular wedding destination, and I could see why.

Devon was outside the showroom, holding a toddler and standing next to a little girl of about three. She waved and pointed to where I could park.

"Welcome! I'm Devon, and this is Lilly."

She waited for her young daughter to shake hands and then continued. "This is Laurel, who is a little grumpy right now, so we'll see how this goes."

"Thanks for seeing me. I'm Sean," I said as we shook hands. Devon was a petite, brown-haired woman with braids doubled over her crown, wearing a peasant skirt and clogs. Not exactly the picture of a realtor I had been expecting.

She led me inside the showroom to a small office off the tasting area. She had built-in, floor-to-ceiling bookshelves on two sides, each stuffed with reference books on wineries, plants, weddings, hospitality and architecture, and all shelved by category and neatly labeled. Her desk was littered with receipts and stacks of brochures, as well as an upturned reference book of some kind. I wondered where there was any room for real estate.

She brushed aside crayons and a couple of loose sheets of drawing paper on a round-top table in the center of the office and set up her laptop, still holding little Laurel on her hip. Lilly took the chair across from her and began to color, a routine I assumed she was used to.

"Pull up a chair over there," she said as she pointed and rocked the toddler. "Nick will be here soon, and he'll take Laurel off my hands for a few."

The toddler stared at me without a smile. I grinned and attempted a little wave, but she didn't respond. She perched on her mother's lap as Devon sat next to me.

"I'll give you the grand tour later, but I wanted to get down to business. I know you're anxious to find out about prices and values in Healdsburg. I'm so sorry about your client."

"I am, too. I was just getting to know him, and I liked him a lot."

"I don't want to pry, but did he die at the property?"

Lilly looked up in a flash and stopped her coloring. Devon ignored it and continued on.

"Reason I ask is that it's a disclosure issue."

"No. We don't think so. He was found on the beach."

"Oh, yes. Nick told me about that. Sorry."

"There is a current police investigation, and I have to wait for their say-so to put the house on the market. But I think they're nearly done with things there. All his possessions are being removed."

She adjusted Laurel, who tried to reach for the keyboard. Devon used one hand to access a website with the stroke of a couple of keys.

"You gave me the address, so I started this preliminary search here for houses with granny units in Healdsburg. Now, you said the front house is rented?"

"Yes."

"Do you think they will be cooperative?"

"I'm not sure. Depends. The husband was initially a suspect, but please keep that under your hat. Not sure I should be telling you any of this."

"You know what? In that case, I'd ask them to move. I don't think you need that kind of baggage when you're trying to get top dollar for the property. And then, we could have it staged, might do a little paint and carpet—you'll be pleasantly surprised with the results."

I thought she was spot-on. I liked her direct and friendly style already.

"That sounds like a plan."

"Have they been there longer than a year?"

"Yes, ma'am."

"So then you'll have to give them sixty days to move. I'd get the paperwork started right away. And just in case, I'd hire an eviction attorney, not that you'll need it. But with you being in New York and the property being out here...let a professional handle it. I have three names I can give you if you'd like."

"Again, you're talking my language. I want to keep it as simple as possible."

"Good."

Laurel was squirming just as I heard the sound of a truck arrive. Devon turned to the doorway. Nick Dunn stood tall and tanned, older, but just as handsome as he was when he was a froglet, though now matured. His blond hair and green eyes were disarming. I'd recognize him anywhere.

"Heard you thought I was an asshole, Sean," he said to me, extending his hand.

Devon giggled, rising with the toddler. "Oh, I couldn't stand him. He was the most stuck-up jerk on the planet."

His arms were strong, hands callused from manual labor with a grip like a bear's jaw.

"Everyone thought you were a royal prick and didn't have a snowball's chance in hell of getting your Trident."

"Well, good to see you, man. Understand you're now a high-powered investment broker in New York?"

"Well, you know, they take anybody these days."

"Hardly."

Devon pushed Laurel into Nick's arms. He planted a kiss on her cheek. "You wanna go ride with Daddy on the tractor, little missy?"

Lilly piped up, dropped her crayons, and ran to her father's side.

"Well, as you can see, these two seem to like me okay. I guess I'm gonna go entertain them so Devon can hook you up." He extended his free hand again. "Again, it's good to see you, Sean. Hope I'll get a chance to do so again before you leave."

"We'll try to set something up. Thanks, Nick."

He left with his entourage.

"You have quite a life here. If I'd thought that guy could run around on a tractor, on a flower farm—"

"Winery," Devon corrected.

"Okay, wedding center and winery—I mean, it just doesn't fit the man I used to know. Good job, Devon."

"Oh, we were a pair, trust me. I think he rubbed off on me more than the other way around. What really changed him was the death of his sister, Sophie. She was very special to him. And she was my best friend."

"I didn't know that."

"She's the only reason we got together. It was a deathbed wish of hers that we date five times before she passed. Let's say the first date wasn't anything like the fourth one."

"I think I get your drift. All the same, happy for you both. Looks like Nick got the brass ring. I think all of us go our separate ways. Most of us don't recognize the people we used to be on the Teams. Except when danger lurks. And then we go right back there."

"It's drilled into you. Nick had difficulty adjusting. Boy did he hate the world. He couldn't see himself doing anything but jumping out of airplanes and snatching bad guys. He loves working with his hands, being out in the open air. We spend most of our days outside, believe it or not."

"Why not."

"Well, we do live in paradise, you know."

I hadn't thought about the island and Ariel all day, and it hit me in the stomach just like I'd been punched. Here was another example of people doing what they loved to do, not what they *had* to do. They were taking chances, throwing caution to the wind, and forging their own trail, not playing it safe like I was. Maybe that's what attracted me so much to Ariel's world—to John's fantasy that was now attaching itself to me. I could feel more of the blue sky and white sand creeping into my bones with every breath I took. I wanted something like this. Like that. I wanted a family. I wanted to work with someone doing something I believed in. It had been hardwired into me as a Team guy. It wasn't loneliness, it was a search for my true calling.

I was looking for love.

Devon finished showing me some spreadsheets and made me a set of action plans that I liked a lot. I had a full list of everything I needed to provide her with to get the ball rolling. I signed a listing agreement but left the price blank so we could figure that out after she previewed the property and we agreed on upgrades or repairs. I authorized her to get some property reports in case something big was lurking, and she included the names of some good attorneys who knew their way around tenant-landlord law.

"I don't want to be unreasonable. I just don't want them interfering. But I'll pay them to leave."

"You tell that to your attorney, not the tenants, okay? Trust me on that."

"I got it. Devon, you sure are on top of things. How do you find the time?"

"These sales are how we're earning the girls' college education. We live on what we make at the winery and save the commissions for our family's future."

As we walked to my car, I knew that I'd met one of the smartest ladies on the planet. Nick had indeed gotten the brass ring.

I couldn't wait to finish with all of this. Because *I* was headed to Paradise.

CHAPTER 17

Pecou was at the point in the investigation where they needed the public's help. It was announced that both Gage and Colgrove had been murdered. He held a public press conference, asking for anyone with any information to come directly to his office. He'd said it was unusual that they did it this way. Most of their crimes, if they ended up solved, were done quietly.

Pecou completed the interviews with the Colgroves' foreman, the surfing instructor, and several other characters who might have had an ax to grind, so he was fairly busy, and I saw little of him.

The property searches had all been completed, so I authorized inspections on the Matheson house, per Devon's request. I also consulted with the first attorney on Devon's list and got the eviction started; although I hoped it wouldn't end that way. I deposited a generous sum into the trust account to pay for all the fees, including a large bonus if the tenants moved within thirty days, which was also something Devon had suggested.

I was itching to get back to New York, and soon after that, be on my way to the island to see if I could find Ariel. I checked out of my hotel, had one more whopper of a breakfast with Pecou at that grill on the square, then turned in my rental car and was on my way to SFO. Pecou insisted on driving me one last time.

He was uncharacteristically quiet, so I asked him what was on his mind. He confided in me that the case was taking a very dark and dangerous turn, as some underworld features to the murders were rising to the top.

"I'm having to be more careful with the staff at the department. I went up to the cabin the day before yesterday and nearly got run off the road by some guy in a big four-wheel truck. I thought I saw him following me back to town, so I hung around the office longer than normal before going home. I'm not going up there again, at least not alone."

"Underworld. You mean organized crime?"

"They're moving in here now that pot farming has been legalized. Think about it. All that money? It's quite a temptation."

I understood all too well about avarice. We had certainly seen a lot of that overseas, people hoarding their meager possessions, killing over a piece of bread. But millions of dollars, that was obviously something that would attract a lot of attention.

"We have people selling out to corporate entities, money changing hands via shell corporations. Threats. You name it."

"So you think John was killed because of that?"

"I have no idea. But my theory is that Barney knew more about the whole situation than someone was comfortable with. I'm just having a hard time finding someone who will talk. The foreman is definitely scared. He's Mr. Low Profile, helpful and smiling all the time, you know? I just get a gut feeling about him. He could be in on it, too. When you employ that many people and make that kind of income, someone is bound to talk to the wrong people."

"I think you're right. Follow the money trail as they say."

I thought further about his words. "You know, Pecou, you need to make sure that Jenny doesn't get muscled. She doesn't have anyone looking out for her."

"I got your message, my man. I'm working on that."

A tiny part of me wished I was able to stay behind and help her make arrangements to move somewhere, at least until the harvest was over.

We rode on in silence. The closer we got to the airport, the more traffic and congestion surrounded us. I felt my lungs constrict as I realized I was about to go back to the tightly packed city of big egos and no privacy. But I was concerned for Pecou. I now considered him a friend, so I had to add my admonition.

"Be careful, man. You got someone who can watch your back?"

He rolled his head from side to side, gave me a smirky grin, and puckered his lips. "More or less."

"Which means, no. You wouldn't have even hesitated if you had someone on your team. Really on your team."

"Well, I don't got a team like you guys had. That's for sure."

"Listen, you need anything, you call on my friends, Nick and Zak. You need backup, and like you said, you can't completely trust anyone in the department, so, you go to them. If you're desperate."

He grinned and slapped my shoulder. "You know I can't do that. Totally against the law, Sean. They'd ride me out of town, or worse, send me to prison to sit and stare at some of those creeps I put there.

"Well, if something comes up off the grid, you let me know. I'd back you up, Watts. And I mean that."

He angled his head. We were at a stop sign just before the pull up to the terminal. "Thank you, son."

"And one other thing. Don't call me son. We're like two years apart for chrissakes."

He threw his head back and laughed. "I was wondering how long it would take you to object to that. Took you a while, didn't it?"

The plane ride back to New York was another non-stop, and I was grateful for the space in first class to lean back and just sleep. My nights had been peppered with visions of Ariel, of course, but sometimes I'd go hours without dreaming. Falling asleep had recently been a chore, not the pleasurable experience it once had been. But this trip back, I slept hard.

My anxiety rose the closer I got to my apartment. When I finally closed the door behind me, I just sat down on the carpet, my suitcases at my side, knees bent, back against the door, and stared out at the view of the Manhattan skyline. This place was my sanctuary, and I hadn't brought anyone here since I separated from Corey. I had purchased everything in the apartment new. Nothing reminded me of my old life. I'd wanted a fresh start. I even sold my car and got another one just so everything around me was brand new and unfamiliar.

Why was that so appealing, I wondered? And here I was again, looking for something new once more. Or was the new car, new apartment, consideration of a new job—although I hadn't acted on it—a failed attempt at finding something else I really needed? Was all this what I needed? John Gage had found it. Nick and Devon found it. I think Zak and Amy did, too. What was I looking for?

In a way, John's walking into my office had changed my whole life. Nothing remained the same. It was all completely unexpected, and nothing I realized I had been searching for. Nothing I knew I needed. But something about this search had planted itself, its long tendrils and roots taking over my nervous system. I wanted to get away from everything around me. It was almost like because I was tending my life, taking care of it, I wasn't really living.

In just the twenty minutes or so of watching the skyline get darker and darker, my nerves had calmed, and my breathing became deep and even. Maybe I was having panic attacks, or fits of PTSD, although I'd never heard of people dreaming about islands and girls and complaining about it to a shrink.

And I'd been lying awake, trying to force the dream to return. I was working at it, trying to push the fantasy back into my life, pulling at it like sucking up something in a vacuum cleaner. But this elusive, incredibly beautiful dream of an island life just floated on by me without landing again. I'd felt loss and pain at first, and then panic, thinking perhaps it was gone for good.

But that was folly. My hands on my hips, I searched the skyline for Superman or Wonder Woman, but all I saw was a police helicopter and a few brave birds that attempted to fly twenty stories high. It was about as far away from a beach as a person could be.

Enough.

I wheeled my suitcases into the bedroom, unpacked, put my shirts and my nice pair of slacks in a bag for the dry cleaners, added the rest of my cotton things to my clothes hamper for the housekeeper to wash, and stowed the suitcases in the closet behind my sport jackets.

I showered, considered going out for a late supper, and decided to keep my morning routine of a run, so I slipped on my other pair of red, white, and blue pajamas and headed for bed. No pressure. If she came, she came. I didn't apply the shave lotion. I didn't bother to comb my hair, just left it in tufted clumps because I felt like it.

I walked barefoot and got a glass of cold water and scanned the insides of my life, as I currently knew it. I decided to tell Ariel why I'd chosen to live this way, just in case she was listening.

I began.

"So, this is the apartment that costs more than I made on my first big job after coming to the city. It's not huge, but in terms of apartments, it's very large." I sidled over to the window and took another cool sip. "This is the view I have of Manhattan. My ex-wife has a better view, but this one is nice. I like it. You can see the waterways and—did I tell you this is sort of like an island? Not like yours, but it is. Just tethered with bridges and tunnels. If you look out there, you can see lots of little islands. There's the Statue of Liberty out there, that beacon of hope and light. I'm sure some see it as a warning, too. Does she look happy to you? I don't think so."

I tipped my head to the side.

"No. She doesn't."

I faced my living room again. "These are very nice leather couches from Scandinavia. They adjust. They feel lovely when you lie on them bare-naked while watching a baseball game and eating popcorn and potato chips. I've only allowed myself to do that two or three times. You see, my Ariel, my discipline is strong. Everything for a reason and purpose. Doing the right thing always."

I glanced down at my toes. "Did you know I care too much about people sometimes? It hurts me. I joke with my buddies, my former teammates, and it's a necessary part of my life to have had that shared experience with so many strong, dedicated, badass guys. But we joke because we die a little inside when one of us doesn't make it home. The laughter and smack talk and needling is like taking your forehead and pressing it against a cool surface after you've bumped t. When it hurts, make it hurt more, and then the pain will go away. Like pressing against leg cramps and breathing into side aches."

I walked to the galley kitchen, taking in the stainless steel and glass cabinets, polished chrome appliances, and a white refrigerator because I don't like smudge marks.

"This is my kitchen. These are the implements of my health," I said as my hand floated through the air, and over the grey marble canister holding my spatulas, spoons, and whisks. "My surgery center. I operate on myself."

I placed the glass on the white Corian countertop. And then realized what I had been missing.

It's you, Ariel. Won't you come and join me? This room has no love. It needs you as much as I need you.

CHAPTER 18

I opened my eyes and saw her standing in the doorway to my bedroom. She was wearing the short, white robe from the hotel in Healdsburg, the ties draped where they overhung to the ground. The front of the robe was open, of course, and beneath it was her bare body, skin latte brown and nearly glowing, as if she were a stone statue buffed to perfection.

She spoke, and for the first time, I could understand her.

"Sean, come here and give me a proper welcome." Her lilting, slightly accented voice made my heart leap. Her eyes danced. Her full lips were barely blushed with rose gloss, making her teeth look blindingly white. I pulled aside the covers and stood, still wearing my red, white, and blue pajamas.

She grinned. At first, I thought she was making fun of my childish nightwear, a routine I could not break and never would. But then I noticed her pointed gaze and realized she'd seen what I just felt: the tent in my pants.

She licked her lips and then crossed her arms. "Are you coming, Sean? Or do I have to wait?"

I was instantly standing in front of her, my body willing to be her tool for whatever purpose she deemed.

Her fingertips softly touched my cheek as I bent down and pressed my mouth against hers. Her gentle moan tethered me further to her web of seduction. I grabbed her face between my palms and kissed her hard, plunging my tongue deep inside her mouth and feeding off her luscious lips.

I was going to say something, but before I got the words out, she pressed three fingers across my mouth.

"Shhh. We have a lot to do before we talk."

I must have looked confused.

"This place needs love."

I wanted to object, suddenly embarrassed by my reveal. She'd been there all along, listening to every word! I took a deep breath, ready to protest, when she put her finger to my lips again, just one finger. With that gesture, I was gentled, reminded that if I spoke, the vision would be lost.

I nodded at her, compliant, ready to do her bidding.

One by one, she unbuttoned my pajama top and then peeled it off my shoulders, restricting my wrists for a bit behind my back as the shirt held me there. Then she removed the top with one flick of her delicate wrist. The one with the bracelet and the red charms. I held her forearm up to me. I realized they were cherries. I kissed the pressure point beyond her palm, then the crook of her elbow, then nipped her collarbone as I slipped the robe off her quivering flesh.

The look in her eyes toyed with my heart while her hands slipped beneath the elastic of my pajama bottoms. Her cool, nimble fingers found my length and massaged it, then reached in further to massage my balls. Her chin was raised, exposing her long, slender neck. As she stroked me, I kissed under her ear and almost whispered something to her, but told her of my desire with a gentle sigh instead.

With her hands on my hips, she kneeled before me and very slowly drew my pants down to my ankles so I could step out. My cock was at her mouth and then inside as her tongue swirled over my skin, the sensation enhanced by her long, rhythmic sucking.

I allowed my fingers to touch the top of her head, and then sift through her strands, the locks smelling of orange blossoms as she pleasured me.

I needed to be mated with her. It had been something I had missed these past few nights. I placed a finger under her chin and then helped her stand before I pressed her body against the entire length of mine.

She let go of my hand and walked over to my leather couch. She sat down, leaned back, and put her feet up on the ottoman. "Like this?" she said.

Before I could answer, she admonished me with a forefinger to her lips. So, again, I didn't speak. I kneeled beside her, pressing her back against the seat of the couch, bringing her knees toward me as I tilted her up slightly higher so I could enter her. Her arms flailed over her head as I lazily moved up and down her nether lips and then plunged in.

The beautiful arch of her back and her expression of surprise and pleasure filled me with flame. I was hungry to be inside, rooting against the walls of her channel, lifting up her pelvis and spreading her knees to accept me. I crouched over her body, watching her beautiful breasts flutter with my thrusting movements, watching her seemingly become over-come with need, touching herself, touching me, pinching her own nipples and then ringing my cock with her fingers and squeezing as I invaded her as deeply as I could. She grabbed my buttocks, digging in her nails, squeezing my flesh to the point of pain.

I pulled out, turned her thigh over in front of me, flipped her to her belly, and then bent her knees, pulling her up. Her glistening peach dripped with her arousal as I sucked her juices and plundered her from behind with my tongue.

She pushed off the couch with her forearms, her smooth ass buried in my face. Her hand gripped my thigh, pulling me forward. My cock slipped inside her tight channel, and I ground my pelvis against her, my shaft impaling her, moving back and forth against the walls of her sex. Our movements became more frantic as I picked up the pace.

I was just about to spill when she turned again, slipping underneath me, guiding my bursting member into her channel once more, and pulling my groin into hers. My hips ground into her, deepening the intrusion, my cock fully consumed by her soft lips, and then I exploded.

I watched her eyes accept me, eyeing my mouth, begging for me to kiss her. I nibbled her, holding my torso over her as my seed filled her. Her internal muscles undulated, drawing me in deeper still.

Finally, I collapsed in her arms.

Again, my eyes opened, and she was gone. I was sleeping face down on my leather couch. My thighs ached, my biceps burned, and my lower groin area was on fire. I rolled over, putting one arm over my forehead and looking at the invisible ceiling, I saw stars in the night sky. I licked my lips and still tasted her sweet juices. My fingertips still smelled like orange blossoms.

I recalled what I had said to her earlier and laughed:

These are very nice leather couches from Scandinavia. They adjust. They feel lovely when you lie on them bare-naked while watching a baseball game and eating popcorn and potato chips.

"Next time, my Ariel. We'll watch a baseball game and eat popcorn and potato chips." I listened but didn't hear an answer. "But I think I like fucking you way better. I dare you to come back and do it all over again."

The room was still, the stars went away. I was in love with the beautiful vision I'd just made love to. She belonged to me in every way possible.

I stretched and pondered our encounter with a smile on my lips. I was satisfied with the thought that I would finally meet her very soon.

"When I talk to you, you aren't going to disappear. I won't let you disappear. I'll convince you to be mine forever."

CHAPTER 19

I kept my morning routine as if I were a clockmaker, the one who made the city tick. The streets were wet in places, steam rose from grates in the curb, and occasionally from the middle of the sidewalk. Inside most businesses there was light. Some metal awnings had been rolled out. Windows were uncovered, and the early morning newsstands were in full retail mode, along with the bagel guy, the pickle seller, and the hot dog vendor.

Everything was as I'd left it over a week ago, and yet it was different. The city hummed and hissed with the promise of new activity. It was a large, lumbering machine just beginning to wake up. I was treading lightly on its seams in the valley between buildings.

I stopped for a quick espresso and then finished my run back to the front of my building. The attendant had now arrived and opened the heavy brass door to the red-carpeted foyer. I slowed to a walk, sipping my coffee as I said good morning to the pretty clerk at the front desk who tried not to look at the soaked tee shirt clinging to my chest.

The etched gold elevator cube made its slow way down, and I rode it back up to my floor as it rattled and groaned as if it too were just waking up. The building had, at one time, been built for opera stars and entertainers at the turn of the century. Renovations had been done without losing the quaint detail of the place. I figured the whole building would rise up in arms if they tried to replace the elevator.

I kept the TV off, opting for music instead, made my kale-blueberry smoothie, and took it with me into the bathroom. I downed the first half of it, then stripped and hopped into the shower, seeking that first cold water on my heated body. I felt great, happier than I'd been in days, and ready to tackle the day. It didn't matter what came at me today, I'd be prepared for it.

It was 6:30 when I strolled into the office, and I wasn't the first one. Our manager usually came in at three a.m. to check the overseas markets, but most of us arrived between six and seven. If you were there after seven, you didn't last long.

I made an espresso and tucked my copy of the *Times* under my arm and headed to my office.

Detective Watts Pecou had been right. The view was out-standing. Light began to shine, casting large shards of yellow-gold between the canyons of buildings. A flock of white and grey pigeons flew a hundred feet down below, looking more like a fallen handkerchief tussled about by the wind. I arched back, heard my spine release a satisfying crack, and sipped my espresso.

I docked my laptop and checked my email, marking one item for a client that apparently hadn't been handled correctly by Sal's team. I'd give him a call at lunch. My sheaf of paper mail was respectable, and I set aside two things to handle today, the rest going into files or the circular bin.

Sal's executive assistant knocked on the doorframe.

"Can I get some deets on your trip to Antigua?"

"Sure. Have a seat." I called up my calendar on my laptop.

"So, Sal said you needed to get there soon. How soon, Sean, because the fares are out of this world for first class. I hope you're being reimbursed for this."

"End of the month, I'm told. So, what are we talking about here?"

"Well, you could leave tomorrow, but it will cost you three grand if you want to go first class with two stops. You can go non-stop in business class for a lot less, like one-third."

"So, when does it start to get reasonable?" I wanted to be fair about the expenses. Three grand wasn't exactly what Roger would call "tight."

"How about thirty days from now?"

I looked at her attractive face with her large, turquoise glasses and answered, "No."

As expected, she blinked and gave me a wide grin.

"Duly noted. So, when does Your Highness wish to depart, then?"

I tossed around a couple of ideas but then couldn't help but think about my session with Ariel last night in my apartment. "Tomorrow doesn't sound too bad."

"That's what I thought. You want the non-stop business class then, I presume."

I nodded.

She made notes, and I watched her pencil scribble across the page. "And the return?" For this, she peered over her glasses.

"Let's give me a week this time. I don't know exactly where I'm going."

"Sean, you're going to Antigua. Where you go from there is your problem."

Not a problem at all, unless I can't find her.

"A week is fine. Thanks, Stephanie."

As she left, I called out to her. "When do I leave?"

"Afternoon, three o'clock. You'll be there in four hours, Sean."

The rest of the day buzzed along quickly. Close to four, which was when I usually left the office, I got a call from Roger.

"Hey, thanks for the death certificate. We just got it in the office."

"Not a problem. Anything new?"

"Well, I got your expense report. You want five grand for an eviction attorney?"

"He won't use all of it, but I wanted to give an incentive to the tenants to move out. We'll need a little to fix the place up, too, but the good news is I found a great realtor, and I think we're going to be over a million in the price."

"Holy smokes. That's close to what things cost here."

"Nearly. It's a house and a granny. Near the square, very desirable for vacation rental, and just outside the restricted area. They control rentals in the downtown area, but it's still just a bicycle trip away. Best of both worlds. Surrounded by huge homes."

"Okay, I think you got it covered, Sean. Send me copies of the listing agreements when you get them signed, and you have the prices firmed up."

"And I'm going to need a little for fix up. Some paint and carpet. Will know more when I get back from Antigua."

"Antigua? When do you leave?"

"Tomorrow."

"How are you planning to find her?"

That reminded me, I hadn't studied the folder sent to me by John.

"I'm tracing from the bank there where John set up the account for Ariel." I knew what Roger would say if I told him about my dreams. Did I expect she'd lead me to her? I half hoped so. Though it seemed real, I still wasn't sure if it was just my active imagination. The meeting in person would be something else, perhaps. I was prepared for that. But I wasn't ready to divulge any of this to a single soul. They would rightly question my soundness of mind.

"Okay, well, I want to hear as soon as you've located her. Best of luck. Get those tickets over to my office, and I'll make sure everyone gets paid back, along with your expenses for Healdsburg."

"Will do."

I got out the bubble-wrapped Priority envelope from John and started to rummage through the contents again. Now that I was actually going to Paradise, I was more focused on what was in the package.

I sorted through the warranty information on the Italian tractor John had bought, the new destemmer, a large, multi-function tool for edging and trimming hedges and turning the soil. There was a list of vendors for purchasing the greenhouses and repairing panels, plumbing, equipment and lists for spare parts. He'd also included a list of the outlets the plants were sold to, as well as the retail dispensaries the product was shipped to.

He had enclosed a brochure for treasure hunters with a list of guides and excursions. There was a shop in Virginia where someone could purchase verified antiquities from the seafaring days of old. I found this to be interesting since the owner had been a crew on several salvage operations in the Caribbean theatre. On the bottom was a brochure for an Inn at English Bay on the island of Antigua. Stapled on the inside of the brochure were two cards. One was for the guest relations manager at the inn, and the other was a private fishing and tour boat captain's card. His vessel was called the *Merrie Me*, and it was available for private charter, parties, and day trips. I was sure John had had contact with both of these people.

I dialed the international number for the boat captain and got a message line, so I left one. I would have sent an email, but he didn't seem to have an address listed. Then I called the Nelson's Bay Inn and got a live person.

"I'm coming to Antigua tomorrow. Do you have any rooms available at this short notice?"

The clerk spoke back in the Antiguan Creole I loved listening to. "You are quite lucky, sir. We have just received a cancellation, so we have a lovely room available for a weekly rental rate of nine hundred eighty-three US." She waited for my response.

"I'll take it. I will be arriving in the evening. Can I hold it with a credit card?"

"Of course, sir. Is this one party or two, please?"

I hesitated. "One."

She asked for my information, and my reservation was complete. "You need car service at the airport?"

"How far is it? I can take a taxi."

"Well, here's da ting Mr. Harper, depending on traffic, it's about a forty-five-minute drive. 'Tis on the other side of the island from the airport. And I'd be very careful, sir. The local taxis are not regulated, not regulated at all. There are some dishonest peoples. I think you should use our car shuttle, sir."

"How much is it."

"It's two hundred dollars US each way, and we require payment in full, round trip."

I knew this was a considerable salary for a local, but also suspected there was a cut that would be distributed through various entities and very little of the price would actually wind up in the driver's hand. But I agreed. I was mentally prepared to take care of the driver.

"He will have a call sign at the baggage claim."

"I'm arriving American."

"There is only one baggage terminal, sir. One waiting area for all baggage claim."

Of course. What was I thinking?

"What name would you like on his call sign, sir?"

Another assumption dashed. Of course, people would sneak away to the Caribbean for a getaway and occasionally not use their real name or not want it announced.

"Harper."

"Very well, sir. We will see you tomorrow night then. Can I offer you refreshments in your room? Are you celebrating a special occasion? Your choice of beverages perhaps?"

"Water. Lots of bottled water, please. Is there a refrigerator in the room?"

"Yes, sir. With or without gas?"

"Excuse me?"

"Sparkling or regular, sir?"

"Oh, just regular. Thanks."

"Very well. I think we are all set. You are sure I cannot offer you discount tickets to the dinner show some night this week? Very lovely, all local Caribbean entertainment. Good photo opportunity."

"No thanks. I might take a chartered boat trip."

"We can arrange that, sir. Where would you like to go?"

To Paradise.

"I'll sort that out when I get there. And one more thing, is Robyn Carver there today?"

"Miss Carver no longer works for us, sir."

"Do you know where I can locate her?"

"Just a moment." She put the phone down and came with the phone number of another hotel on the island. "Not sure she is still there, but she asked her calls be forwarded there. We have a much nicer property, Mr. Harper. You won't be disappointed."

"No worries. I plan to enjoy it. Thanks very much. See you tomorrow."

I tried dialing the number I'd been given, but it was disconnected. I found the hotel name and a different phone number for the Blue Water Suites Hotel on the internet, so I dialed and asked for Miss Carver again. The operator stated that she was on her days off and would return tomorrow.

So now I had two more people to contact. I checked the names of the two Antiguan bank managers from John's instructions, made a photocopy of everything, and left the originals in a file with Roger's information locked in my desk.

Before I left the office, I checked in with Stephanie, obtained my confirmation information, and gave her instructions for some of my client follow-ups for Sal.

"Not sure I'll be in tomorrow because I need some things for the trip."

"Pack your sunscreen. Should be hot this time of year," she cheerily said.

"I hope so. Say, I was wondering if you could look up to see if any of the access checks have been used, you know, the ones we set up for John Gage?" I gave her the account number connected.

"Hmm. Let me check. You want me to close the account?" With a couple of keystrokes, she was able to report to me that yes, one check had been cashed, in the sum of ten thousand dollars.

"Ten thousand? All in one place? Did he open up a bank account with it?"

"Nope. It was cashed at the Sugarloaf Casino and Resort in Hopland."

"Where is Hopland?"

"I've no idea, but it cycled through Bank of America in San Francisco, so I'm guessing it would be someplace in northern California."

"I've never heard of it." Then I recalled seeing signs for a couple of Indian gaming areas along the freeway. "I'll need a copy of that check. Can you make one for me?"

"Sure." When she returned, she added, "You know, those casinos are often run by gambling interests in trust for the native tribes, just like here and, well, all over now. Ten thousand dollars is not a large amount of money to them. Especially when the funds can be verified. And these certainly could be."

She was right.

"So, do I close the account?"

"Nope. There might be more coming. Would you check in a couple of days and if more come through, send me copies by email?"

"Certainly. Have a great time, Sean."

Armed with my little file of paperwork, I left the office, confident that I was getting closer to uncovering the mysteries of John's past life, and the life he'd intended to have. We were trained to calibrate most everything if we had three points to plot. I had four, not counting my dreams, which I gave as much weight to as all the others combined. It wasn't typical SEAL thinking. No one would ever believe me.

It was my heart guiding the way. I was ready for whatever was to come.

CHAPTER 20

I was grateful a well-tanned, older, hippy-looking man occupied the seat next to me. He sported a white-haired ponytail and wore Bermuda shorts and flip-flops. He wasn't interested in any of the scenery and attempted to sleep the whole way.

But I was keyed up. I regretted not giving Pecou a call before I left New York, but vowed to do so when I landed. I was confident that if anything urgent had occurred, he'd have left a message or emailed me, so I didn't worry about it. My hands tapped the armrest on my left as I peered out the window. As I left the mainland and crossed over the Caribbean Sea towards the little islands of my destination, my anticipation grew. I tamped it down, aware that it was a mistake to overthink things. Just like in the BUD/S training, there was no way to figure out everything that might come at me. I just had to have the confidence that I could handle it, whatever it was. If I had expectations, I'd be distracted and perhaps not able to think straight enough to survive the onslaught.

I chastised myself for thinking about this adventure like a mission. But there was an element of danger to it all. Just a different kind. Murder in the US was a very serious matter. Here I was, the bearer of good news and bad news. I sensed that Ariel would not be happy with the bad news of John's death. And she wouldn't be happy with the news about the money either because of that death. If I set my expectations low, I'd be in better shape. She might not want someone to console her, no matter what my dreams intimated.

Get prepared for rejection, froglet.

But my heart was screaming in the corner to have hope. Hope was a dangerous thing. The aircraft's wheels touched down hard, and it shot my pulse sky-high. All of a sudden, I was there, in closer proximity to her and the island John had talked about, one step closer to the discovery of the mystery of his decisions.

At the very least, I would be a winged messenger, showing her the lighted path to a certain golden future—if she chose that. She wouldn't have to stay on the island. She could live and travel anywhere she wanted. She would nearly have enough money to build a small resort on the island if she wanted to, a place of continued employment for her family if she so chose. I thought of many opportunities for her to consider. I'd work with her until she understood what had been left for her and what her options were.

The terminal was oppressively hot, and within seconds, I was brushing up against other sweaty bodies and smelling some ripe odors. The lilting Creole chitchat I heard sounded like the chirping of large sea birds. I had to concentrate to figure out phrases. I saw more gold teeth, piercings, beaded hairstyles with colorful headdresses, and cotton fabrics wrapped around large and small bodies than I ever had before. It was a clash of cultures as several groups of Japanese tourists in white pants and identical navy blue jackets emerged and were given first shot at the swirling baggage kiosk as they chattered away like a flock of seagulls.

I had brought just one bag. I had one suit, just in case I had to do something official, but had mostly packed shorts and my hiking pants that zippered in three places, giving me multiple lengths. I brought my favorite pair of worn-in leather sandals and a couple of pairs of slip-on loafers that could double as dress shoes. I had every bright, short-sleeved aloha shirt I owned: three. And threw in a nice golf shirt I'd bought in Healdsburg with an abundance of white tee shirts. My boxers were all red, white, and blue and, of course, I brought my pajamas. With luck, everything had survived the trip and would not need an iron.

I pulled my bag behind me and found a crowd of people held back by what looked more like cattle guards. There were lots of eyes trying to get my attention, to sell me things or offer a car and tours as I scanned the crowd. But above the sea of heads was the sign with my name on it, and that made me rest just a tad easier.

Cecil was nearly three hundred pounds, which was of great help maneuvering us through the crowds. When I lagged behind, he reached around and took my suitcase, pushing it out in front of him. The shout, "Move!" was quickly heeded by everyone nearby, and I found the crowd parting like the red sea.

It was a cacophony of sounds and smells, the lilting music of steel drums, laughter, clapping of hands, and singing and shouting—sometimes sounding the same. A group of Antiguan singers was screeching with great enthusiasm, and in perfect rhythm, if not in tune, bidding us welcome to their island paradise.

Cecil stopped in front of one booth. "Here. My gift to you."

The booth advertised a coconut liqueur with free tasting, but I wasn't going to turn down a gift, so I took the little brown shot glass and threw back what was in it. The sickly sweet liqueur burned all the way down, but had a decent vanilla aftertaste and didn't taste chemically altered, so I just let it wash over me. I saw a flash of turquoise and red out of the corner of my eye, but it quickly disappeared.

"Dis is island original drink. My sister, here, Sarah, she gonna pour you another, and you take it, okay? You can buy her bottles. Makes herself in her own kitchen."

I wasn't sure why he thought that was a selling feature, but I was game. I'd come armed with money I was happy to spend to loosen tongues, get information, and try to relax on my mission to Paradise.

"I have pound cake. Coffee, vanilla, or chocolate. I tink you like the chocolate, sir. My own cake." Sarah's words sounded moist, and I soon discovered why. She had no front teeth.

"I'll take a bottle and two pound cakes."

This created a loud shout of applause from Cecil, who let everyone in the terminal know that I was a buyer and I instantly knew I'd made a mistake. Vendors started to flock to me, dangling wooden snakes, voodoo dolls, and straw hats with yarn dreadlocks already attached just so I "could feel like one of the locals." There was no fuckin' way I'd wear one of those.

I must have looked lost, or perhaps Cecil thought my purchases might interfere with his tip, because he strong-armed people, pushing them away as he shouted. Sarah grinned with her gums and handed me my plastic bag with my two pound cakes and my very large bottle of local liqueur. I'd only meant to buy the little one she'd held up.

I handed over my sixty bucks in three twenties because I didn't understand the local denomination or the price. Her fingers gave me the come-on for more money, and I put another twenty on her palm. She did it one more time, so I gave her another one and indicated I was done. I did expect change, but she was off to give a sample to another tourist.

Now one hundred dollars poorer and only about five hundred feet from the gangway of the airplane, I waddled behind Cecil, who had now placed considerable distance between us. I was now worried I'd never see my suitcase or my ride again. But I was wrong.

Cecil hauled my suitcase into the trunk of his black Crown Vic like any experienced baggage handler, and I was seriously impressed. He had to bang the lid several times before it finally latched.

"Go, inside. Too hot."

I agreed with him, took my valuable prize, and sat in the back seat, scorching my ass. The car cooled down as soon as

Cecil revved it up. We were off in a cloud of smoke, nearly hitting a group of school children crossing the parking lot holding hands. He honked at them, and they scattered to the sides.

He passed me his card. "You want to go anywhere on dis island, you call Cecil. I am your personal guide to my beautiful island kingdom."

"Thank you. So you've lived your whole life here on Antigua?"

"No. I was born in Brooklyn."

I raised my eyebrows.

His head whipped back, and he gave me a hearty laugh. Even Cecil had gold teeth. "My mother came back home. But I am a US citizen. Good for me, right?"

I nodded, not sure what to say.

"So, do you go back to Brooklyn very often?"

"Never been. Some day. Maybe I rob a bank or win the lottery." He laughed again. He must have been enjoying himself exposing me to his "Island Kingdom." I figured he was used to either scaring or impressing well-meaning and bashful American tourists. I knew the brotherly love was partly genuine. The brochure I'd read on the plane said the country's greatest export was its people. The unintended assumption could be taken to mean they were doing human smuggling or running away. I chuckled over this.

Truth in advertising.

I was anxious to find the beach, the blue water, and the island relaxation I'd been seeking.

The temperature fluctuated between freeze-my-butt and bake-my-butt all the way to the top of the grade where Cecil pulled over to another *sister's* cart selling tropical drinks and brightly colored shirts.

"Dis is the finest material in all the islands," Cecil's considerably older sister said, showing me by rubbing the cotton fabric between her gnarly fingers.

"I can see that. I've brought my own."

She frowned and looked at Cecil, who shrugged. "Dis woman has a very very hard life, Mr. Harper. She has a sickness with her children."

She looked to be well beyond childbearing age.

"How many does she have?"

"Eight. Very very bad. She lives in a house no bigger than this shop."

I thought that was probably true, based on the various plywood shacks roofed in rusted, corrugated metal sheets. Along the way, young boys brought pieces of building materials up the hill, a piece of wood here, a piece of metal siding or roofing there, sometimes balancing several items on their heads as they walked barefoot beside the dusty roadway.

Who would know if I bought something horribly ugly and bright red, right? I pointed to the shirt closest to me, with the label clearly telling me it was made in Sri Lanka, and I got a different patterned red shirt in a plastic package, folded and pinned.

"Ah, very nice. She give you her special shirt. Brand new. All clean."

I certainly hoped so and passed her a twenty. She did not ask for more and gave no change.

"You like memento of the island, I have necklaces, and beads for your woman?"

The array of plastic string holding the red, yellow and green colors of Jamaica, some with the familiar marijuana leaf symbol on them, or the painted rocks with the letters Antigua hand written were of no interest to me, and I passed on all of it.

"I'm fine. Thank you. Just the shirt is all I need."

Cecil took off again, leaving behind a cloud of dust falling all over his big sister.

At the top of the mountain that had created Antigua, probably from an old volcano, the views were stunning. Blue water outlined in white sandy beaches could be seen off and on in between residences great and small. Well-manicured estates sat right next to a row of shacks no larger than the estate's garage. Resort signs with names like *Blue Coconut* and *Turtle Bay*, even one called the *Nutty Irishman* dotted the hillside. There wasn't an abundance of tall trees, but several large colorful plants I'd consider houseplants in New York stood in the ground and topped more than two stories.

The colors were so bright, I soon grew mesmerized with everything vying for my attention. I'd never seen so much turquoise and bright pink. Children and pets, including goats and pigs, wandered along the gutters of the road, hardly taking notice of us.

Cecil was on his cell phone shouting an order I couldn't understand. When he hung up, I asked him about the resort Miss Carver worked at.

"Dat on the other side of the island. You want me to take you there first?"

"No. I was just wondering. About how far is it from the Inn."

"Oh, dis one? Oh, it's about forty to forty-five minutes. Long way."

I thanked him and went back into my reverie. It was hard to imagine a quiet place on the island. I'd not experienced that as yet. But I had hopes it was coming very soon.

At last, we passed through a regional park, manned by a uniformed young lady in a park ranger uniform, which must have been swelteringly hot. Down toward the water's edge, I saw a little conclave of single-story buildings made of stone and wood. Beyond the tiny city center was the Inn, looking just as the brochure had depicted it, covered in red and green vines, a grand cobblestone entrance and porch extending out front to greet us. What I could see beyond the Inn was an array of incredible sailing ships—something I'd seen in Monaco and the south of France—and yachts that defied description. Groups of two or three well-dressed tourists mingled, pointed at the boats, and sipped wine. A grand lawn extended from the back of the Inn nearly to the water and was peppered with occupied and abandoned lounge chairs. I was looking at something very old, scenery that probably hadn't changed much, except for the boats, in a couple of hundred years.

The plaque on the side of the front door to the lobby said the building had been built in seventeen seventy. Inside the foyer, a light breeze blew through the open windows as I walked the old plank floors, stopping at the front desk. The courtyard garden off the restaurant and sitting area was sunny and inviting.

The sound of my suitcase literally being jackhammered to submission by Cecil's huge arms as he dragged the case over the cobblestoned walkway broke the allure of the moment. I gave him a generous tip and promised I'd call if I needed transportation.

The woman at the reception desk called a porter, a teen-age island boy, who struggled with my case up the switch-back flight of stairs to the second floor. With a stunning view of English Bay, I walked out onto the balcony through large, oak double doors. I tipped the boy and locked the room door behind me, anxious to shed my travel clothes and do some early exploring. The sun was beginning to set, highlighting the sleek white boats and their tall masts. A wooden jetty was at one end, farthest from my view, and boasted a couple of local vessels, one looking more like a ferry. I scanned the two carefully. On the back of the one on the left was the name,

Merrie Me.

CHAPTER 21

I didn't worry about the shower, the unpacking, or hanging up my suit. I grabbed a bottle of water and took off down the stairs, racing out through the lobby, watched by several people. I didn't care what they thought. This was my shot to get ahold of someone here who might have seen or talked to John Gage.

I turned the corner and briskly walked in a direct line across the lawn. Two lawn chairs were vacant, facing the bay, a bucket of long-necked beers between them. A man with a baseball cap was wiping down the handrails and polishing chrome. He wore jeans, a ridiculous flowered shirt like the one I'd bought at the airport terminal, and faded canvas slip-on shoes. His hair was graying and frayed at the temples where it stuck out from under his cap. Most of it was bunched into a ponytail, the strands medium brown and curly. His moustache was full, also laced with gray. I figured he wasn't originally from the island, and he appeared to be ten or so years older than I was. But his arms were tanned and well developed, so he could have been retired military or police. He looked more like a cop.

"You the owner?" I shouted out to him.

"Yessir. This here's my rig. I was expecting two of you, but you're early, and I like that." He flipped on lights.

"Oh, I'm not the paying customer, but I wanted to ask you about hiring you for some sightseeing."

"No problem. I got lots of time. Nobody coming in after tonight until Saturday. Where you figuring to go?"

His accent was southern, but I couldn't place where. I searched the lawn area behind me and didn't see anyone on their way over, so I continued.

"I'm actually looking for an island. Something out of the way, private. Maybe not on any map?"

He stopped wiping down the rail and stood tall for just long enough that I could see his physique. It gave him away. He was former military, all right. He was playing down his strength by slouching over a bit, after forgetting himself, so I did the same.

"I'm Sean Harper. Former SEAL Team 3. Were you Special Forces?"

"You're pretty good." He wiped his hands on his cloth and jumped down to the landing in front of me, extending his hand. "Billy Quarles, Team 5. But I only did ten. You?"

"You got me beat. I only did six." My hand was still pulsing from the grip he'd put on me, in case I didn't think he still had it. It was then and still was our measuring stick.

"You guys got to see some action then. We were the ones watching you from the Hotel Del with our umbrella drinks and our ladies, thinking we'd been born too soon."

"Yeah, but some of you guys were mean instructors. And you saw your share, too. You were South America?"

"Pretty much. Grenada, Columbia, you name it."

"Well, brother, I'm going to be honest with you. I'm looking for a gentleman who had your card in his personal effects. He had stories about an island, a girl, and a white sandy beach."

Quarles examined his fingernails. "Personal effects. That doesn't sound too good."

"I'm afraid it's not." It was beginning to darken. "Can I ask you why someone would want to go out on the bay tonight?"

"They have a fireworks display around the point for one of their carnivals. Real pretty on the water at night. I just take them out, we have a few beers, and then I bring them back. Someone's idea of a date, but it's a special occasion, I'm told."

Just then a young couple came up behind me.

"Captain Quarles?"

"Aye, me hearty!" Quarles answered in pirate dialect, winking at me.

I stepped back and allowed them to step up on board the boat. Quarles leaned over to me. "I'll be back in about three hours. Meet me in the bar, and I'll answer your questions."

"Sounds good, man. Thanks."

We shook again, and he resumed his stage performance. I heard the young woman giggling and asking questions as they set out into the mouth of the bay. I waited until the lights of the *Merrie Me* were no longer visible.

I returned to the lobby and took at look at the bar area. There were several groups of friends scattered about. I deduced that they were people who rallied at the bay, owners of the large, expensive charter boats. I'd seen posters of a regatta going on sometime later in the month and knew this area would be overrun with people in a few weeks. I was glad I'd come ahead of the crowd.

I ordered a rum punch, suddenly feeling like I should get with the island pulse. The drink nearly knocked my socks off it had so much alcohol. The bartender barked at me.

"You okay?" He sounded more like the pirate in the room than Quarles.

"I'll thank you once my sinuses clear."

He humphed and slipped over to help another customer. I took my punch, left the bar, and went upstairs to my room.

Across the bay, I saw lights flickering here and there from islands I had not yet been able to see. The breeze coming onto shore was delightful, warm and just like I'd imagined it in my dreams.

I turned to begin my task of unpacking, shaking out my crumpled suit and hanging my slacks. I folded what I couldn't hang up, setting out a pair of Bermuda shorts and the bright shirt from the airport. Since we were brothers, I figured we might as well look like brothers. And we'd both be wearing red.

I stripped and jumped into the shower. The water tasted rusty and wasn't particularly hot, but I was grateful for the clean wash just the same. Besides, cold showers were never a problem for me.

I dried off and sat at the padded bench outside on the balcony wrapped in my towel, placing my forearms on the metal railing caked with layers of paint. I tried to remember the last time I'd stayed in a place that was built around the Revolutionary War. I was feeling the history of the island, much of it bloody, swarming around me. I was touching things that Admiral Nelson had perhaps laid his hands upon. Maybe sleeping in a room where he'd taken one of his many mistresses.

I'd read he hated it here and I couldn't figure out why, except at that time he'd been a man of twenty-eight, at the beginning of his military career. At thirty-five, I was ten years past mine. I didn't make the lifetime commitment to travel clear across the ocean, which exacted its share of lives and consumed men every day. He was probably anxious to be in some kind of battle or skirmish, rather than forced to babysit some English slave owners and their plantations. He was a border guard, sick with tropical diseases that dogged him his whole life. He wouldn't have known of the illustrious career he'd someday have.

Was there some kind of fate like this awaiting me? Not nearly so grand, of course, but was I about to embark on something that had already changed me? Something that had already consumed John Gage and Barney Colgrove? I didn't want to be in the middle of a firefight. I came here to experience what it would feel like to run away from the world. I did not come to prove myself. I'd already done that. I could make a living in one of the most desirable places in the world, and yet I was looking for something more. Was on a mission to fulfill someone else's dream of rewarding someone with opportunity.

This place was an intersection of time and opportunity. It meant different things to different people. To some, it was a stopping place on their jaunt around the Caribbean, hauling pleasure tourists or running races. To others, it was home, a place to work, to provide for their families. For Admiral Nelson, it was a place to languish and yearn for excitement, battles, and great victories at sea. For one woman, it was a place of waiting, seeing who would come across the watery void to bring news of someone she expected to spend the rest of her life with.

For men like Quarles and me, it was a place to provide service, fulfill other's missions and dreams, with the hopes that perhaps, one day, there would be a dream we could partake in. Holding on to hope that something more was out there, somewhere.

I was waiting for Billy Quarles when he returned. When he spotted me in the corner, bracing myself against the wall after my third rum punch, he made a gesture as if my shirt had blinded him.

"I see the hucksters got you, too."

"I've never owned such an ugly shirt in my entire life. When I get back to New York, I'm going to give it to the first homeless guy I meet."

Quarles thought that was funny. Since I was at a mental disadvantage from the rum, I was glad, because I didn't trust myself.

He bought a beer and joined me.

"So. John Gage. You know John Gage," he said.

"Did. Yessir. I would have liked to have known him better."

"So, what brings you here, then. I take it he's passed?"

"He left instructions in his will. I'm supposed to find his Ariel."

"You think she really exists?" Quarles was dead serious.

"I saw a picture of her. You mean, you haven't met her?"

"Never did. I took him over there probably a half-dozen times. I even stayed over one night. Very rustic. Not much there. It was an old campground owned at one time by some bigshot from Texas. He built cabins on the island for his hunting buddies, and I guess he had plans to make it his private game preserve. Tried to import things they could go kill."

I could see the captain wasn't a hunter. I had never understood the fascination with it either. I'd hunted men, and there was some philosopher who'd said something about what happened to you after you hunted men, but I couldn't recall who it was. I wasn't even sure I heard Quarles correctly.

"So, this isn't some untouched place no one's ever lived on before?"

"John tell you that?"

I scratched my head. "Dammit. I've come all this way to talk to you, and now I fuck it up by drinking too much punch." I was royally irritated with myself.

"It's the place here. This place changes you. You'll see. Lots of ghosts in the islands."

"He owns the island now. He wants to leave it to her."

"I'm not surprised. The way he talked, she was a real beauty. He promised there would be a wedding, and I'd get an invite. Was kinda looking forward to that."

I was starting to see shadows outside, people walking inside or back out to their boats. People were saying goodnight. Quarles was right, the island was changing me even as

I sat there. I wasn't sure if I saw things from my imagination or things that really existed.

"Look, Sean, I'm sorry about John. I liked the man, and I was pulling for him to spend his days in paradise."

"That's the name of the island, Paradise."

"No, it's not, Sean. Locals call it Fish Island because of the shape. I think it looks more like a jellyfish than a fish. But if John owns it, and I'm not doubting him because he was totally set on living there the rest of his days, then he owns it. I'm not going to doubt him."

"I saw the deed. He does own it."

"Then we both agree." He leaned in closer to me. "So, I say we go out there tomorrow, and you and I can have a hike, walk all around the island and see if we can find your Ariel."

"She's John's Ariel."

"Except John's not here. And you are. Judging from that look in your eyes, the same one John had, I'd say she's your Ariel now. Let's go find her, okay? We'll solve this mystery together."

CHAPTER 22

Quarles said he lived down the road, and we agreed to meet at nine in the morning, although I'd suggested earlier.

"Gives you some downtime with rum and the girl, Sean."

I watched him saunter away, his gait casual but everything else anything but—the tats, muscles, and formidable bearing evident despite what he tried to show. I wondered if he'd been having these wet dreams about Ariel, too. Maybe there was such a thing as some island muse that overtook unsuspecting men. Gage was certainly an overly trusting soul. I was vulnerable, too. That could explain some of it. But Quarles? He looked about as hardened as a man without a family could be at mid-forties. I should have asked more about him, but I had been so eager to get started, we made our plans, and that was that.

I needed a burger and a tall glass of water after the long talk and too many rum punches. I watched the dwindling crowd. Nearly everyone except the waitstaff was over fifty, retired men and women of means I was used to catering to in New York. This place really was a playground for the rich and powerful.

I walked outside and decided to just soak up the breeze that blew in sounds of steel drum music from other areas of the islands, perhaps traveling over the water to come to me. I was excited about tomorrow.

A young, blond woman walked along the row of some twenty-million-dollar yachts, casually perusing the names written on the sterns. She wore an island wraparound dress I saw everywhere, her shoulders covered with a bright scarf or wrap. She stopped at the *Merrie Me* and lingered. Then she turned and came back my way.

"Have you ever seen such an impressive lineup?" I asked her before she could get away.

She was startled. I guessed she hadn't seen me.

"I'd say. Way out of my league." She began to walk away and then stopped. "Is that your boat?"

"The *Merrie Me*?"

"Yes."

"Nope. But I'm meeting the captain here tomorrow morning at 9 o'clock. You're welcome to join us."

"That's okay. Heading back to St. John's tonight. I'll catch him another time."

"Who should I say wanted to speak to him, then?"

"Not important at all. He doesn't know me."

I could tell she wanted to get away quickly, so I let her go. "Good night, then. Be safe, and let the wind guide you."

She startled, then gave me a warm smile from what I could see of her face, nodded, and disappeared into the shadows. I waited a reasonable amount of time, then walked back through the lobby and caught a glimpse of taillights headed down the narrow, cobblestoned drive leading to the main road.

I climbed the stairway, anxious to get some restful sleep. It was near midnight and had been a long day. I left the windows open since it was the same temperature outside as it had been three hours earlier. The air was welcome, and I figured the music would lull me to sleep. I put on my red, white, and blues, and went to bed, anticipating my big adventure the next day.

She was there again. This time, waiting at the beach. The *Merrie Me* pulled up, and Quarles whistled when he saw her.

"John was right. A real beauty!"

"I didn't ask him to come ashore, just jumped off the boat into near waist-high water and walked in. A second later, a canvas tote bag came flying through the air, landing to our right on the shore. The sky had turned dark, and it was just past dusk with stars beginning to appear.

Ariel didn't pay any attention to the bag or to the boat. "You're back!"

I was about to say something but slapped my own palm against my lips, which drew a grin.

"Good boy," she said in her island accent. "You are learning, Mr. Sean Harper."

I turned back toward the bay and saw the *Merrie Me* motoring out into the Caribbean Sea.

She was next to me with her arm wrapped around my waist like it had always been there. I smelled the orange blossom scent of her hair. "You want de grand tour?"

Of course. Show me where you live. I want to see it all. I was being careful not to speak.

"How much time do you have, Mr. Sean Harper?"

I have the rest of my life.

A cloud hovered over my heart as I vaguely remembered something I was supposed to tell her. But my proximity to her body was distracting.

We walked in silence, me holding the canvas bag over one shoulder, my arm linked with hers as we walked hip-to-hip through the sand until it turned to grass. Torches were lit in a meadow-like area surrounded by palm trees. A large fire was blazing in a firepit at the center, bordered by large tree stumps for sitting. Beyond the meadow, I could see the outline of a small shack with a thatched roof. It looked just like the ones I'd seen before.

What is this place?

"Our family compound. You cannot see it, but my family lives over there through the jungle, a little bit up the hill. But this is my house."

I searched the green tangle of foliage around the perimeter, looking for signs of light, listening for voices. All I heard were the birds calling, echoing throughout the jungle, with the sounds of the ocean crashing behind me, now muted.

Her home was lit by candlelight. It was made entirely of local timbers and woven fronds and grasses, lashed with straps of hemp and flattened bindings made of other plant material. The floor was littered with woven mats. A couple of large upholstered chairs draped with bolts of colorful fabric sat side-by-side facing the doorway with a small table in front, laden with a large bowl of unusually colored fresh fruit I took to be local fare. In the corner, her bed was a bundle of pillows and covers of various sorts, again in brightly colored fabrics that looked to be hand-painted.

"Where is your kitchen?"

And...she was gone. Everything was gone, including the island, the torches, and the fire.

I lay back and tried to bring her back, but I was too tired. The mixture of travel, tropical ocean moisture, and alcohol had taken its toll. I set my mental alarm for eight o'clock, figuring that would give me time to dress and catch a light breakfast downstairs, and then just accepted the fact that sleep was what I needed.

Just before I drifted off, I heard her voice, "Sleep, Sean Harper. Come back to me tomorrow."

Quarles met me at the boat. I'd expected to see him come through the little restaurant and at least share an orange juice with me, but he stayed away. I'd been watching the couples and crew coming from the Inn, mingling with the boat owners. A TV set blared in the corner, tuned to a business channel with stock market indicators. It was unlike me to not even take notice of what was going on in the world back home, but a handful of people were glued to the screen, some making remarks, and others laughing.

I finished my black coffee and joined Billy at the *Merrie Me*.

"Morning, Sean. How you feeling today?"

"I can't complain."

"How's your head?" he said as he gave me a hand to step up onto the boat.

"Actually, I'm better than I thought I would be. Slept like a baby. Just what I needed."

"That's good. I brought some Bloody Marys in case you needed them. But the rum actually gets into your blood system fairly quickly, and you begin drinking it like water after a time. I see you're adjusting quite well."

"I am. I think I love it here. Like I've lived here my whole life."

"Wouldn't go that far, Sean."

He cranked the motor, tossed over the lines, and we were out into the bay in seconds. The sky was bright blue, the water a brilliant turquoise. I put on my sunglasses and realized I'd not brought a hat.

"You got an extra cap?"

Quarles reached into a compartment under his seat and threw me a Yankees baseball cap and a tube of sunscreen. "I come prepared."

"Yankees? How did you know?"

"Don't flatter me. Brought it from home.

As we headed out into the open waters, several green islands appeared. All of them were flat, some not larger than an atoll. Occasionally, a house with a dock and a boat could be on one, but the area was literally peppered with them.

"You wanted an island not on any map, well, none of these are. Any big maps, anyway. Local maps have them. There are hundreds of them scattered all over the place here."

"I had no idea. Are all of them inhabited?" I had to shout so he could hear me.

"Some. Not all, though. Some are owned by people who probably don't exist anymore." He winked and then threw his head back and laughed. "Ghosts of the Caribbean."

"You mean pirates."

"Not anymore, or not like in Disney or anything. The kinds of pirates we have are farther out at sea, and they're all bad guys. All of them. That's why these owners travel in pairs or quads. Kind of dangerous these days out there. They stay in constant communication with land or each other. Only stupid people go out alone or go too far. Those are the ones who don't make it back," he boomed over the sound of the motor.

After an hour, Quarles slowed down. It made conversation possible.

"So, Sean, today we're headed east, and a bit north. We've got probably another half hour to go. You want to explore any of these islands, do a loop around anything else today before we get to Fish Island?"

"Anything to see?"

"Lots of places I could show you to fish or snorkel. I can show you some old shipwrecks, beaches for just chilling. Sometimes, I bring people out and then pick them up later on. You've hired me for the day, so whatever you want."

"Oh, I almost forgot." I reached into my pocket and gave him the three hundred dollars we'd agreed on. "Sorry I didn't give this to you earlier."

"No worries. If you didn't pay, I'd just dump your body overboard and let you sleep with the fishes."

His follow-up belly laugh irritated me. I realized I'd just come all the way out here without a prayer of being able to swim to any nearby shore, knowing nothing about the man or his real background. I wanted to know much more about him all of a sudden. I decided to be direct.

"So, Billy, being out here alone with you isn't exactly a laughing matter, and your comments are putting me on edge. Can you tell me why that is?"

He shut off the motor and let the boat drift. His seat was higher than mine, and as he looked down on me, he removed his glasses.

"Be careful, Sean. Life down here isn't as idyllic as it seems. We're civilized, but just barely."

I studied him, my apprehension building, but I was confident I could handle myself, as long as he didn't have a gun. I kicked myself for not packing mine.

"So, what's your part in this fishbowl of a place?"

He faced the open sea, put his glasses back on, and sighed. "I keep my eyes and ears open. I make enough money to live, and I try not to piss off the wrong kinds of people so I can stay here."

"So what am I?"

He turned around again, and once more removed his glasses, leaning closer toward me, his elbow on his thigh.

"You're bait."

CHAPTER 23

"So, you ready for that Bloody Mary yet?"

He must have seen the way my body tensed. He wasn't a stupid person, and if he'd meant me harm, *real* harm, I'd be dead. Another lesson learned. Maybe I'd been off the Teams too long. Getting soft. Not paying attention. Why did I think that just because I wasn't over in the Middle East it wasn't still a dangerous world out there? I knew this. I knew I had to say something, but all I would be able to do was listen to his next move.

"So, I could tell you've been itching to tell me something for the past hour, Billy. I just didn't expect it to be this."

The water was calm. I was floating in the middle of paradise, not John's Paradise, but a place where the whole world would want to be nonetheless. And yet I wanted to be anywhere but here, sitting on this guy's boat, soon to learn my fate and see if there was anything I could do about it.

He put his glasses back on, adjusted his seat, and leaned his chin on his hands supported by the wheel.

"I didn't know you were a Team guy. I wasn't told that."

"Told by whom?" I couldn't help the bitterness creeping in.

He shrugged. "The people who hired me."

"And who are they?"

"Some bad guys. Hired like me. Except they lied to me."

"So what's the plan, Billy? What is it you want?"

"Not me—"

"The hell it's not. You supposed to take me out here and 'dump' me like you said? There's a whole paper trail and a handful of people who know right where I am. You want some of my brothers on your tail for the rest of your life? Not that it would make a difference to you. I can see you're bent."

He delivered me a sneer.

"You're not being very smart, Billy. You know you aren't."

I could tell he was thinking about something, but I knew I wouldn't like hearing what that was. But there was nothing I could do except wait. I had no means of getting ahold of a single person. I could fight him off, head back to shore, but then what? Tell someone he threatened me or fell overboard and take my chances in Antigua? I needed to know who else was involved in this little floating Bloody Mary party.

"Come on, Billy. Talk to me. What the fuck is going on here?"

"Look, you got to know I didn't know you were a Team guy, honest—"

"Oh, cut the crap, Billy. That has nothing to do with it. Tell me what the fuck is coming down. You owe me that at least."

"I was just supposed to deliver you to the island."

"To the girl?"

"They don't know where the girl is. That's why they need you. You were supposed to be taken to the island. And that was all I was supposed to do."

"Who are these people?"

He removed his glasses again. We'd floated into a current of some kind and the water began to get choppy.

"I got into a jam. Left the States hoping for a new life like John Gage. I was discharged from the Teams. *Dishonorably* discharged. I didn't get my ten years in. I have a gambling problem. When it got too big, it blew up everything there I cared about. Wife, my job. I tried to do several things for work, but I just couldn't get out from under the debt. So, about two years ago, I came here to start over."

"So, lots of people leave the Teams. I've known guys who got into trouble. It happens. What's the deal?"

"Borrowed some money from a small-time guy here, bought the boat, and business was going good. And then John Gage showed up about a year ago. I thought I was helping him, until I found out he'd come with followers he didn't know about."

"Who were they? Would you just fuckin' tell me, Billy?"

"They said they were from the Treasury Department. Feds of some kind. They were tracing illegal money laundering. I know there's a lot of that going on here. John didn't look like that kind of guy, but these guys scared me, so I agreed to cooperate."

I didn't want to give him any information on John at this point. I was just going to listen and feel grateful he wanted to talk. I'd make the determination if he were telling the truth later. I already rated him as untrustworthy and a total scumbag.

"Go on."

"I just thought I was agreeing to tell them about what John was doing and where he went. For that, they offered to give me a substantial sum so I could pay down the boat. I told them I didn't want to get involved in testifying or any witness protection thing, and they said no problem. They wanted me to help them keep tabs on him, and weren't going to hurt him. I got the impression John was doing something illegal, trying to disappear, or at least that's what they thought."

"You really believe they'd actually pay you thousands of dollars for information? Government agencies don't do that, you asshole. Wasn't that a red flag?"

"Look. I didn't want any trouble. I just wanted to get the boat paid off and be left alone."

"And then what happened?"

"I started listening to John. How he was going to leave everything behind and just live here with his woman. I guess I believed him. It was the same thing I wanted. And then he told me about buying the island, not just visiting it. I guess I started to like the guy."

I'd felt the same way. I was pulling for John. Thought he was naïve, but pulling for him. Billy had apparently felt that, as well.

"They told me someone would be coming to try to locate the girl. That's all. Said you were enabling him to move some of his money, both of you were in on it, and they wanted to catch her."

"So you expected me, then."

"Yes. When you showed up, that's when I found out he was gone."

"Not gone. *Murdered*. I was in New York, said good-bye, and the next thing I knew, I got the call he'd been killed."

The vastness of the horizon, a shade of bright light blue against turquoise with nothing in between was so serene and stark. Dangerous.

"So, what's the plan, Billy?"

"I fucked up. No question about that. I don't blame you for not trusting me. I used you, and that's my shame and baggage. Let me just apologize—"

"Asshole, I've had about enough. Problem with you is you've gotten so used to making excuses and asking for forgiveness, it doesn't mean anything. No one can count on you, and if they're smart, they don't either. You think they don't know they got you dangling by your balls?"

"So that's why I'm telling you all this. I put you here, now I want to help you fix it. I don't know if these guys are anything but local punks. The real guys are the ones who hired them. I'm guessing they are from the States and I've never talked to them."

"Oh, so now you have second thoughts? Not really about doing the right thing, is it? You seriously think I buy your horseshit? Wouldn't it have been better if you had told me before we got the hell out here in the middle of the ocean?

I was looking for something I could hit him with, something I could break on his precious boat. But, of course, that wouldn't be very smart. It was my fault I was in this position. Nothing was as it seemed. I felt like I was finally waking up from a coma and living some fantasy place I had no business going. There was no checking out for me, no going off to some idyllic island somewhere. And maybe John didn't agree with that either. I was a man of action, and right now, I needed to get control of the situation.

"So, where does this leave us, Billy?"

"We have a couple of choices. I take you to the island. I don't know what awaits you there, but I'm guessing it's not good. Or I can take you back to English Bay and the Inn. Though you might want to get out of Dodge while you can. Or, we think of something else."

He didn't know I had knowledge of banking transactions in St. John city, things I'd sent there for deposit. As far as I knew, that's where a good chunk of John's cash was. I needed to somehow reach Ariel without drawing the attention of the predators on my trail. I was hoping they didn't know about all the accounts I'd set up. Somehow, I needed to figure out who I was dealing with.

I considered Roger's involvement. Did he have something to do with this scheme somehow? I really didn't want to go there.

But going to Paradise, or whatever the island was called, to meet Ariel was not happening today, and maybe never would. Something else was happening.

Ariel was the real target, and if I weren't smart, I'd lead the bad guys right to her.

CHAPTER 24

We got back to the Inn around one o'clock. I packed as quickly as I could, examining my things to look for signs that anyone had gone through my stuff, but everything looked intact. Perhaps that's what they planned to do once I was delivered to the island.

I called for the driver and was annoyed when they told me it was Cecil's day off.

"You are leaving us so soon? Was there a problem with your stay?"

"Not at all. It turns out something back at the office has to be handled today."

"Where are you going, Mr. Harper," the pretty reception clerk asked, batting her eyelashes at me. I was immune to everything now. Fear was just on the periphery of my eyesight. Anxiety made me check everything out. My vacation and fantasy trip were over.

"Need to get down to the airport. Expecting a package," I lied through my teeth. "Anyone else who could take me, or do I have to get a taxi?"

"Oh, that would be very expensive."

I considered what might be said if I spent big bucks on a taxi, knowing it would give a signal in this tiny village that would be easy to pick up.

"Where's the biggest hotel on this part of the island, something with a fax machine and a business office?"

"Oh, that would be the Carlisle, up the road about ten minutes."

"Can you get me a cab to take me there?"

"Mr. Harper, we have a fax machine and a copy machine."

"I know. I just need access to a computer to send off some things back home."

A red and white, fairly clean taxi showed up about ten minutes later. As I suspected, he'd been over at the bigger resort.

Before we drove away, I searched for Billy but didn't see him. We'd decided the best story was that I had pressing business back in New York and that I was leaving the island but would be returning in a few days to explore further. We agreed that none of our conversation about what would await me at the island or anything else would be discussed. He was just going to wait at the Inn and let them come to him, which I agreed with.

The road was bumpy, just like I remembered it. I was relieved to see a string of taxis waiting in line for pickups in front of the palatial lobby of the Carlisle.

"You are checking in? Dis is very nice place, much nicer than the Inn," the driver informed me.

I let him take my bags, handing them to a doorman, gave the driver a tip, and thanked him for the ride. I followed the white-gloved doorman into the lobby.

"I need to go to your business office first, please."

He pointed down the hall and offered to store my bags, but I declined. Soon, I was in a very nice room equipped with computers, fax machines, and supplies of every sort—and privacy! I asked for some computer time and access to a telephone to place a call to New York. I paid in cash, declining a room charge. My thought was not to use my cell phone for anything so that my calls would be more difficult to trace, in case a government entity was involved.

First call I made was to my office. Sal wasn't available, but his assistant was.

"How's it going? We're all envious. And thanks for not posting pictures, Sean."

"Thanks. Look, there's a chance I'm coming back early. I've checked out of the Inn. Not sure yet where I'll be staying, but I was wondering if you could find some flights back to New York maybe tomorrow or the next day?"

"Sure. What's going on?"

"Well, I'm gonna have to leave that for Sal. So, have him call me, okay?"

"Sure thing. Are you all right? You're not getting sick, are you?"

"No. Just some developments I didn't anticipate. Can you tell me if there've been any inquiries about John's accounts or the estate over the past few days?"

"Nothing that I saw. But I can ask Sal to give you a call. He might have heard something. Been pretty dead around here. Oh. Sorry about that."

"No worries. Text me the choices on flights home, okay? I'll let you know where I'm staying. Will Sal be back tonight?"

"Sean, I don't think so. It's a board meeting day, and sometimes they go long. I'd guess he'll call you in the morning. But I'll work on these flights before I go home. Look for something from me in the next half hour."

"Awesome. You're a peach!"

"Bring me back a handsome pirate, and we'll call it even."

I hesitated to call Roger.

"Sean! How is Paradise?"

"Not what I thought. I have to make this quick. Is there something going on with John's estate that I need to know about?"

"Like what?"

"Roger, I just need to know if you've told me everything."

"God, you sound uptight. What the hell's going on? There's not much to tell. I just met John twice. Spill it."

"Appears some people are after him, looking for the girl, and now, looking for me."

Roger was quiet for a moment. "I have had a couple of calls from Sonoma County inquiring about the land there. The farm and vineyard. I told them it was a private sale as far as I knew and directed them to the County Assessor's office."

"So they know John sold the property?"

"Yes, I told them. Both calls. One had the name of the trucking company, so I verified that, as far as I knew, that was who now owned the property. Geez. You thinking you're in some kind of trouble?"

"Would the Treasury Department be involved? FBI maybe?"

"Well, they usually come walking in here. Not usually done by phone, unless I'm getting a subpoena for records. Trust me, the Feds don't act this way. I'm the attorney of record, so it's not uncommon for people to inquire, especially in a death case. Realtors looking for property to sell. But, heck no. No one told me they were from the FBI or anything. That's a little creepy."

"Okay, well, I've moved and am looking for another place to stay tonight. I think I should get back home."

"What about the girl and the island?"

"Not at all the dream and vision I imagined. And I have it on good authority that she's not there and probably hasn't been. Listen, I'm going to call Detective Pecou and see if he has any suggestions. I sure hope he does. And I don't have to tell you, I don't much care for being here all alone."

"So, you think the girl is in danger?"

"I do. And the widow owner of the ranch. Just found out about all this a little over an hour ago. When I get more, I'll let you know."

"Sean, please do. You want some company, some help?"

"I hope I don't have to ask you that, Roger, but thanks."

I hadn't considered the possibility of getting Roger involved, but now that I thought about it, the idea was strangely appealing.

Next call was to Detective Pecou. His cell went right to voicemail, so I left a message.

Hoisting my bag over my shoulder, I walked to the lobby area, out to the bell stand, and requested a cab. I was placed in line behind two elderly women, and within five minutes, was on my way to St. John's. I still had the picture of Ariel and the addresses of the banks that were the contact for her, but I doubted they'd give me much information. It was still worth a try.

The white pillars of the Swiss-American National Bank made me feel like I was touring some Egyptian tomb. The floor and countertops were all done in expensive Italian marble. With the bright shirts and dresses of the bank employees, especially the ladies with their headdresses, everything was in stark contrast, like living inside an ice cube.

I introduced myself to the bank manager and showed my credentials as executor of the estate of John Gage. The accounts were set up so either Ariel or John could use the funds. I asked him if he'd ever seen Ariel and showed him the picture.

"Pretty girl. I'd remember. I'm sorry, Mr. Harper. Our account information is confidential, and your paperwork doesn't cover it. Maybe if you get a local attorney, he could help you—"

"No, you don't understand. I just want to locate her. This is the only address I have on file."

"I understand, but even if we had another address, I don't think we can give that out. I could check, if you wait right here."

I took back the photograph and had an instant change of heart. "No, thanks. Can you tell me if the funds arrived? If she was able to take possession of them?"

"No, I cannot give you that information. As the sending party, wouldn't you have confirmation of the transfer?"

My little ruse wasn't working. I thanked him, left my card, and wrote my cell number on the back of it. "Would you mind giving her this if she comes in?"

"I'm sorry, Mr. Harper. I may not be the person she talks to here. I can't be responsible for this." He tried to hand back my card.

"Just keep it, then. If you see her or want to give it to her, I would appreciate it."

I walked the six blocks in the late afternoon heat, and by the time I was at the Bank of Antigua, I had sweated through all my clothes. I considered changing my pants to my shorts in the restroom.

I set down my canvas bag, pulled out Ariel's picture and my papers and began to walk toward the bank manager's desk. A blond woman walked right in front of me, cutting me off as she headed for the row of tellers.

It was the same woman I'd seen last night at the harbor. I took a chance.

"Ariel?"

The woman turned and stared at me, her eyes wide, her forehead creased. I could tell I'd totally surprised her like I'd done last night.

"You're Ariel?"

She quickly glanced to the right and began to slip out the front door of the bank.

"Wait. Please. I'm John's investment advisor." My voice was wavering, I was so nervous. She was not an island girl, and I knew from speaking with her last night that she didn't have a local accent. She was from the States.

"I need to talk to you about John. It's urgent."

Stopping in place, she bowed her head and nodded, letting me approach.

"I'm very sorry to have to tell you this, but John is gone. He died in California over a week ago now. I've been instructed to give you the balance of his estate that he left in trust for you. Ariel?"

I bent forward, trying to make contact with her down-turned eyes. When she raised her chin, her eyes were filled with tears. She let them trail down her cheeks with no other expression.

"You are going to be a very rich woman, Ariel. This is what John wanted. He loved you very much. But there is more. You've been followed. I think you're in danger."

Her gaze clung to my eyes like I was keeping her from falling into an abyss. I placed my hand around her forearm but didn't pull. "Please, can I get you something cold to drink? I'll explain it all."

She nodded. Just as we left the bank building, she whispered. "I was afraid of this. He didn't show up. Does this mean he died in an accident, or—"

"Come." I took her hand, and we crossed the street to a tiny café with bright turquoise shutters in disrepair. The sounds of Caribbean drumbeat music infused the air. I pulled out a chair for her, caught the attention of a waiter, and sat across the table.

"It's still being investigated, but yes, all things point to murder. As much as I'd like to take a long time and tell you the whole story, I'm afraid we don't have that luxury, Ariel. I fear the same people who went after him are here, in the islands, and are working very hard to find you."

"I want to see proof you are who you say you are."

Just then, two men wandered in through the front door and took stools at the bar in the corner. One of them was on his cell phone. I watched them peripherally, but something triggered my instincts. I knew their indifferent glances over to our table were anything but casual.

"Come on. We have to go." I grabbed her wrist and didn't give her a choice.

We dashed out the front door and ran down a narrow alleyway behind the bar. In a manner of seconds, the two men were running after us, one shouting something I didn't understand. Shopkeepers and children watched us run past them as they hung out in doorways. People peered through second-story windows, following the chase.

We turned another corner, and I hastily opened a screen door, which led to a kitchen filled with Chinese cooks, who began screaming at the sight of us zigzagging around their boiling pots and large, smoking woks. I was pummeled with wooden spoons, and a woman shrieked, shouting at us in Chinese. We exited the dining room filled with curious tourists, collided with a woman carrying a large tray piled high with dishes, and escaped through the front door onto a one-lane street that was buzzing with scooters. We ran up several storefronts into the next alleyway and into a side door, finding ourselves in a laundry. Huge machines in rows were tended by workers amongst a couple of barking small dogs and a chicken, of all things.

I veered around the two-legged beast, nearly pulling Ariel to her knees. She was dragging, and it was impeding our progress, so I stopped, repositioned my canvas bag to hang around my neck in the front, then hoisted her up on my back and ran with her arms around my neck and her legs jutting out at the sides. At the end of the block, I saw that the laundry was, in fact, the ground floor of a very nice hotel. The first door was locked, but the second was open. We were in a food service area with stacks of knocked-down tables, bins of silverware, and stacks of folded, white tablecloths.

"There has to be a service elevator here somewhere," I said, catching my breath, yanking on her legs to make sure I didn't snag her on something that would send us flying. I was pacing myself, like carrying the two hundred pounds of rocks on my back in my combat boots. Ariel was so much lighter than that, but still I pushed myself. An alcove and double doors leading to banquet and meeting rooms passed us, until finally, I saw the red *Elevator* sign and pushed the metal button with the upward arrow.

The doors lumbered so slowly, I was sure I'd see a beefy arm or some large menacing body impede its closure, but finally, we were alone in the cab, and for now at least, safe.

I almost forgot she was on my back, so I let her slip down, being as gentle as I could. She adjusted her clothes and leaned against the back wall with her right hip and then took in a deep breath, letting it out with force.

"Wow."

"You okay?"

"Me? You just ran a five-hundred-yard dash through the back streets of St. John with me on your back being chased by bad guys. We almost turfed a chicken, turned over pots, and nearly exploded with noodles and tofu. Yet you managed not to step on a child, a dog, or a woman.

I was trying to catch my breath, was totally soaked with sweat, and finally had to lean over bracing my hands to my knees so I didn't get dizzy.

"You sure you're okay?" She placed her hand on my shoulder and bent slightly to be eye-level with me.

I stood up, and she dropped her hand. I could see she was on sensory overload, as her eyes scanned my face and upper torso. It was hard not to feel the weight of her realization that I was built like a brick building, even at my age. And I was grateful to show it.

"Where were we?" I said, still having difficulty breathing as the motor rumbled and the cage scraped the sides on its trek up the floors to the top.

The elevator doors finally opened to a hallway of rooms. I walked toward light and looked out a large window overlooking the square where the bank was located. We could see two large men resembling the ones who had chased us, wandering back and forth in the square and hanging close to the entrance to the bank.

"Pretty sure we're safe up here." I looked down at her, and she was staring back up at me.

"What?"

"I've just never seen anyone run like you did. I think you're the strongest person I've ever met."

"I like to stay in shape. It's a way of life for me. We got into the routine, and for me, for many of us, it just sticks."

"What do you mean?" she asked.

"I'm former special forces."

"No wonder. An advisor who kicks butt."

"I believe you were going to ask me to prove I'm working for John."

"Yes. I want to see something John gave you that shows you were hired to work for him or his estate."

"First . . ." I pulled out my papers showing John's will. Before I handed it over to her, I held them to my chest. "I want to see some I.D."

"Mine?"

"Yes, ma'am."

She dug for her wallet and produced a California driver's license.

"You live in California?"

She shrugged. "Sort of."

I examined the license showing an address in Palo Alto.

"You *sort of* live in Palo Alto?"

"My things are still there, but—" She put her hand over her mouth. "Dammit, I want to see some proof you are who you are."

I showed her my military I.D., the one with the gold Trident superimposed over it. Then I produced my New York driver's license. Her eyes swept from side to side as she studied both of them.

"This," she said as she fingered the Trident, "this means you are or were a SEAL, right?"

"That's right."

She wouldn't look me in the eyes. Angling her head to the side, she asked me, "Do you have anything with John's hand-writing on it? Something that proves you at least met with him?"

I thought about this for a few seconds, and then I remembered the photograph—the one I'd thought was Ariel. I pulled it out of my manila envelope and handed it to her. She flipped it over.

My Ariel. Queen of My Heart.

Tears spilled over her cheeks again. "This is Tawny. My roommate from college. He wanted a picture he could show people, just in case—" She dropped the paperwork at her feet, kept clutching the photograph, and hugged me. With her head smashed into my chest, she whispered, "Help me. Please, help me. I have no one else I can turn to."

CHAPTER 25

I let her get her panic out of her system. Rubbing the back of her neck with one hand, my other kept her close as she sobbed, then sniffled, and then pushed away from me. Her eyes were red, and her cheeks and neck were blotchy. I thought a little logistics and a plan would help her with her nerves. Nothing worked better for me and my fear than designing a tactical maneuver and then carrying it out.

"Where are you staying? I asked.

"Last night, I stayed out by the airport. I was going to go back there."

"Anything valuable in the room? Anything you need?"

"Well, my makeup bag, and of course my clothes."

"I'd recommend not going back there. Call the hotel and have them send your things to my address, and I'll forward them to you. I think it's possible they were watching you."

"Could have been following you," she suggested.

"Entirely possible. But let's not take chances. We're here now, and I'll go down and get you a room. You need to get some rest."

"Where will you be?"

"I'll try to get a room next door. How about that?"

She nodded. I was careful, placing a palm against her cheek. "Don't worry, Ariel. I'm not going to let anything or anyone hurt you."

There was a meeting room at the end of the hallway that had still not been cleaned up. Bottles of water and bagged snacks were left behind from a morning group.

"You wait here. I'll come get you." Before I left, we exchanged cell phone numbers. "I don't want to use this except in an emergency. But if I text you, please do what I ask, okay?"

"Sure."

I registered for a one-bedroom suite, which would give her privacy and me a comfortable couch to sleep on. The great thing about Antigua, they didn't blink when I chose to pay in all cash, and there was nothing to sign. I gave the clerk a fifty-dollar tip.

In the gift shop next to the reception desk, I purchased a wraparound dress, a long-sleeved tee shirt, a pair of drawstring pants, and a travel vanity bag with a toothbrush. On my way back to the elevators, I passed a business center with an International UPS symbol, and another bank of computers and fax machines like at the Carlisle.

I found Ariel asleep, hunched over the boardroom table, softly snoring. I picked her up, and although she struggled at first, she threw her arms around my neck and tucked her head under my jaw. I opted for the service elevator again, just in case, and one floor down, we were in our room.

"Listen, I ordered some things. If you want to go take a shower, I got you a little travel kit and some temporary clothes." I handed the bag to her.

"Thanks." The distance between us was awkward.

"If you want something to wear to bed, I can lend you these." I took my red, white, and blue pajamas out of my canvas bag and tossed them at her.

She cracked the first smile I'd seen all afternoon.

"Go shower, and then we'll have some supper."

I knew she had to be exhausted because I was, as well. The emotional roller coaster was probably taking a toll on her. There was a lot we still needed to discuss, but perhaps tonight wasn't the night. Just as promised, the room service was quick, and I had ordered extra bottles of water, so I downed one before she came out of the bathroom.

"What do we have here?"

I had to laugh because she looked ridiculous in the pajamas, which were nearly falling off her. She rolled both of her sleeves up nearly ten inches and sat down.

I'd ordered fish and chips and some batter-fried jerk chicken and two salads. She ate like she hadn't had a meal in two days. I found myself shoveling it down, too, as I hadn't had anything since breakfast.

"So, Ariel is your real name, then?" I asked as I handed her a wet washcloth for the messy, bright orange chicken sauce.

"Yes."

I thought it was time to tell her how much she'd inherited. So far, she'd never even asked. "Ariel, you're a rich woman."

"News to me."

"What you're inheriting is substantial. Seriously, John had me deposit a huge sum into your account at the Bank of Antigua. You are also the owner of a large investment account at my firm, and a note secured by real estate in California. We think he has some cash somewhere, possibly on the island, we haven't been able to find. But we will. All this was left to you."

"It feels like blood money to me. It isn't mine."

"But he wanted you to have it."

"He wanted us to enjoy it. I never wanted to live here without him. This place scares me, and now with all this money...it scares me even more."

I was glad she felt that way. Not that I was expecting it, but I didn't want to see any greed coming from her side of the table. I planned to play my role exactly right down the middle, the honorable way, the way John would have wanted me to. No more wet dreams and stupid fantasies. The constraints of my job were kicking in, and I was going to conduct myself in a manner above reproach.

"Well, it is yours to do with as you please. If you still feel that way after some time, then donate it to a cause you believe in."

"Having too much money is a big responsibility. I've never been attracted to that sort of stuff. Look what happened to John—just as he was about to enjoy himself."

"Didn't you know he was wealthy?"

"Yes. He told me. I wasn't really sure whether to believe him at first. I finally had to tell him not to talk about it. I have no interest in money. Really, I don't."

I sat back, flabbergasted at her response.

"You should know how much he left you, a lot of it is in cash."

"I'll probably see a statement at some point in time…"

"You'll have to sign that you received the funds."

"No problem. Then I will."

"Something else you will have to consider—just because it isn't important to you, doesn't mean it isn't important to someone else. That makes you a target."

"See, I told you!"

"But you can't just ignore this. We have to get you to safety."

Her eyes welled up again. "That was the idea of the island, a place where no one could find us. We would just drop off the map. Enjoy life on life's terms. Try to get by with a garden we tended, spring-fed water, maybe some propane, a generator for some things, but generally off the grid. No visitors unless we wanted them. No phones or internet. Our place."

I was still thinking how incredibly naïve the two lovers had been. John had very nearly gotten her killed, as well.

"You can still do that."

"No. It's too dangerous." She wiped her cheeks with the backs of her hands. "I'm sorry, but I'm kind of a mess."

"That's understandable."

"So you brought everything with you, all the stuff I have to sign?"

"Yes, I did. And you have enough money to hire a crack security team. They can shield you from anyone who wants to get too close to you. You need to find a place where you can rest at night and not feel like every little noise is a prelude to an attack. Someplace fenced, with alarms, possibly guards—"

I stopped because she was looking at me with a horrified expression. "That sounds like prison."

"It's what people do to keep themselves safe. Do you know how many people would attempt to kidnap you for your money?"

"Not if they don't know."

"Ariel, that's not very smart. Someone knows. John was killed. The owner of the property he sold was killed. What makes you think they won't resort to a third murder to get what they want?"

"I thought you said the police were on top of it."

"They are. But they can't be everywhere. Did John mention anyone in particular he was concerned about?"

She shook her head, started to pick at another chip, and then pushed it aside.

"So, what do I do?"

"What do you want to do? You have choices now. First thing needs to be your safety, though."

"I understand."

I placed the tray outside the door and pulled off my shirt. She was sitting on the couch, legs tucked beneath her, watching me. I instantly felt a little self-conscious. There was no masking how she openly viewed my naked chest. I pulled the shirt to me.

"Listen, I'm going to shower. Why don't you head to bed? I'll borrow a pillow, but see if you can find me an extra blanket, okay?"

"Okay."

I was headed to the bathroom when she called out my name.

"Sean?"

I turned just in time to feel her slam into me, holding me as tightly as she could with her arms wrapped around my waist.

"Thank you," she murmured into my chest. "I'm finally starting to feel safe."

It was such a little thing, but something I'd not heard in nearly ten years. How could she know that hearing those words would melt this former SEAL's heart? It also cemented my calibration. My only job was to get her to safety, and then get out. Just like on the Teams.

CHAPTER 26

After my shower, I put on a pair of red, white, and blue boxers and surveyed the living room. She had put a folded blanket and pillow on the couch. The door to her bedroom was ajar. I briefly checked on her and found her sawing logs. I was amazed that such a pretty lady could make such disgusting noises while she slept.

I closed the door, spread out the blanket so I wouldn't have to feel the scratchy fabric of the couch on my back, punched the pillow a bunch of times, and laid myself out. My feet stuck out from under the blanket, and that would be a problem since the air conditioning was on.

I opted for turning the cool off, opening the slider just a crack for some decent air. The steel drum music seemed to flow twenty-four seven, just like the rum and the undercurrent of mystery and danger, but I preferred that sound to that of an air conditioner.

On my back, I stared at the ceiling. No stars tonight. Probably no visions of the island girl, whoever she was. Thinking about all that had occurred, I knew now that my wet dreams and visions must have been some delayed reaction to all my life-changing decisions. Right after the Teams, I'd gone straight into the investment training program and a life in New York because that's where Roger had wanted to go, and that's where I'd met Corey. Those two set my course, and I just followed along. Then I got entrenched in the Manhattan thing, the job, the company, and, frankly, the money. It was a good life, but it wasn't really the life I wanted.

And then John had walked in that day. It was like he was some magical trickster bringing his bag of wonders to throw at me, filling my head with stories and desires I never knew were there. He triggered in me an urge I'd stuffed down after being out of the service—the desire for adventure. Throwing caution to the wind, like I did when I joined up. It wasn't about being a SEAL or having all the cool gear or training, it was just jumping out of the airplane of life into a new realm. It was the unpredictability that attracted me.

Until gravity caught up. With my feet on the ground, I knew there was a price to pay for everything. The dangers of the real world came back into focus. Evil men and evil deeds were everywhere. They were in Afghanistan and Yemen, as well as New York, wine country, and the beautiful islands of the Caribbean. There was no escaping the fact that if people had something truly miraculous, no matter what it was, someone else was hell-bent on taking it away. Some wanted to steal it. Some wanted to spoil it, some just enjoyed taking it away. If we stood for anything in this world, there would always be those who saw us as targets and took aim. Like it was said, they only had to be right one time. My vigilance would be forever tested.

So, all of a sudden, I was here, in a hotel room, in the islands, helping a beautiful young woman sleeping in the next bedroom take charge of her life and her fortune, with no plans or hope to participate in any of that except to get her some-place safe. It was what I did, and now, it was what I was doing.

The steel drums lulled me to close my eyes, and I began to hear the jungle birds.

Enough. Let me sleep.

"Good-bye, my Sean. I'll see you in another lifetime."

I was barely aware she'd been standing over me as I sat on the beach and watched the sunrise of a new day.

I was awakened to a bright room and a buzzing cell phone.

"Pecou, my man. How're things in Sonoma County?"

The detective was a warm welcome back to the real world. "I'm fine. But how be you? Had your fill of palm trees, Voodoo, and those nice things that run around half nekked?"

"It's beautiful here. But I'm finding that danger lurks everywhere. No such thing as paradise."

"The island, or the concept?"

"Both."

"I got hauled to too many churches in my young days back in N'awlins, and those snake charmers done put the fear of God into my young ass. My maternal grandmother spent half her time rolling down church aisles and shaking the devil from her bones. I liked my mama's concept better of a nice, peaceful place with just a little jazz. Something beautiful and quiet. I was hoping that's what you'd find there, Sean."

"You think it exists?"

"Well, let's just say this. I knew if anyone was to find it, it would be you."

The reason for my call flooded back into my head, and I got serious. "Watts, if I can still call you that—"

"Go ahead."

"I found Ariel."

"That's good."

"And I'm trying to keep others from getting her. Some people I think from your area have followed me here."

"That's bad."

"I've managed to evade them, and we're lying low in a hotel for now. But I have to get her out. I can't leave her here. She really has no one."

"She has you, Sean."

"Well, for now she does. But Watts, I'm playing this by the book. This isn't about anything but her safety. I was hoping you could give me some suggestions, and perhaps get me up to date with the investigation back there."

He exhaled, and I could tell he was smoking a cigarette.

"We've arrested the foreman. God knows how they'll handle the harvest now, but we had to move Jenny to your friend's place, your lady friend who is the realtor?"

"Nick and Devon's?"

"Yes. I convinced her that she was living in a cave with a bunch of bears coming for her. For her own safety and the safety of the kids, I got her to move, thank Gawd. She's got some sorting out she has to do."

"Okay. I'm glad she'll have a couple of ex-Team guys nearby. I like that."

"As long as they don't meddle."

"They won't unless attacked."

"I got that."

"So you think the foreman was the murderer?"

"Nope, but hoping he'll roll on someone. Just arrested him yesterday. A guy like that, one who has a big mouth and talks when he gets drunk is usually not smart enough to engineer a plan past a day. Jenny reported he'd been threatening her."

I agreed.

"Jenny's livelihood is not my concern, but I believe Devon and your friends are hooking her up with someone who is reliable and can help. We're working on some things, and I think we can squeeze the foreman to give up his real bosses. They tried doing this before. Fingers crossed, Sean."

"So why would they come here to the islands? I mean, if they have control over the property, or will get it somehow, what's here is just some bare dirt in the middle of the Caribbean Sea and some cash. What am I missing, Watts?"

"Don't you remember you thought it could be a lot of cash? Plus, your little lady owns a note that encumbers that property, right?"

Then it came to me. "If they get their hands on the note, or get it signed over to them, they will have control of the property."

"In a roundabout way, yes."

"So, what do you recommend?"

"You know as well as I what to do next. I'd get her out of there, like you said. Bring her back to New York, or someplace she wants to go. Some place where we can control the environment. Doesn't she have any relatives?"

"I don't think so, but I haven't gotten that far."

"They do things differently there in Antigua, and I have no contacts. I'm just another citizen as far as they're concerned. You've got to get back to the States and quick. Something happens, I can't reach out and get you out of trouble, Sean. You can't hide out when you don't know who you're hiding from."

He was right. I needed to be on my own turf.

I heard the sound of the door to Ariel's bedroom opening. She stepped out, nearly tripping on the pajama pants. She had her kit with her and pointed to the bathroom. I nodded.

"Okay, I'll let you know. I'll see if I can arrange that. I'm not making outbound calls, just so you know."

"This is a secure line. They won't find me here."

"Sounds like you're doing all you can."

"It's a waiting game now. We'll get them. I never give up."

"I'm the same way."

"Say hello to Ariel. Someday, I'd like to meet the little lady who started this whole thing."

I heard the sounds of the shower as I hung up. Checking my text messages, I found three from Stephanie. After not hearing from me last night, she'd texted again later to give me more times for today and then tomorrow.

Just let me know when you surface, loverboy. And did you find the pirate yet?

I scrolled over the flight times. There was an early afternoon flight that we probably wouldn't make. There was a non-stop red-eye to JFK tonight, and both were available in first class. And there were flights available tomorrow. Three of them.

Just then, Ariel came out of the shower wearing the wraparound scarf-dress I'd bought. It looked wonderful on her. Flowers in pink on a background of turquoise like the ocean.

"You look great," I whispered.

"Really? Come on, Sean, these colors look like they belong on a sixty-year-old romance writer, not me."

All I could do was shrug. "They didn't exactly have a big selection. I was trying to get something that would fit and not fall off you."

"And no one will miss seeing me, either. It's a neon sign that says: *tourist.*

"Well, you are a tourist, Ariel. So am I. We just bring some baggage is all."

She finally gave me a brief smile. That was two. "Are you hungry?"

"I am."

"Order some things from room service while I shower. And then we have to talk, get our strategy outlined."

"You want coffee?"

"You bet. Eggs, whatever you're having." I retreated to the bathroom and left her to make the call. While in the shower, I thought about the paperwork I had with me, some of it things I needed her to sign for the estate. They were replaceable, of course, but once she executed some of them, it would close the last loop on the transfer of the estate to her. Perhaps they would be dangerous in the wrong person's hands.

Roger had said not to let them out of my sight, and here I'd been running down alleyways with bad guys after us, those documents in my canvas bag. I could have been overtaken, and everything lost. I decided I was taking too many risks. We should have set it up so we met at someone's office, or at one of the banks. But knowing Roger, he trusted me and assumed that no matter what, I'd get them signed and returned to him.

I heard the door open to the hallway, and Ariel talking to the person making the delivery. I quickly opened the door, and the waiter stepped back in alarm. Ariel was signing the room tab.

"No. I'm paying for that," I said as I grabbed the black order book and removed the tag. In my shorts, I still had a fifty and some ones and gave him the contents. "Rest is for you." I handed him back his empty book.

When he bowed and left the room, I waited to check on the door latching, put my finger to my lips, then listened and quietly opened the door to peek down the hall. I got a glimpse of him turning the corner to the service elevator and was satisfied he was who he said he was.

Ariel looked worried. "So, what was that all about?"

"You're not using your head, my dear. You have to distrust everyone."

"I didn't know how much cash we had."

"I do. And so would you if you'd go to the bank and get it."

"I have a credit card."

"Which you won't use while here. I don't want any way for you to be traced. And please don't use your cell phone."

"But I already have."

"Who did you call?"

"I called home. Told my girlfriend I'm coming back after all."

This was new. I kicked myself for not laying down the ground rules more clearly. "Dammit, Ariel. That's my fault, but seriously, do not use anything electronic—anything—until we get things figured out. Your life is on the line here.

She nodded and plopped herself on the couch, crossing her arms like a petulant child.

I knew what she was thinking. "It isn't like prison. We're just not in a safe place. Just let me do my job for a few hours, then when—" I hadn't even discussed going home tonight or tomorrow. "So you've decided to go back to California?"

"Yes."

"Let's do an orderly exit, so you make it. It's that serious. I don't mean to be harsh, but you have to listen to me and do everything I say."

She angled her head and pouted her lips. "I've never done everything a man has wanted me to do."

I could have taken it as the sexy come-on it was, but I pushed it aside. And she was right, too. I doubted she'd ever followed anyone's instructions. She was a dreamer, living a life people like me had died to defend. She had no idea what kind of danger she was really in, or how bad people could be. And I knew too much.

"Ariel?" I said, lowering my voice and taking her hand, pulling her up off the couch. I could see the expectancy in her expression. "Time to eat your breakfast before your eggs get cold. And we have to have a little chat."

I pushed her shoulders down, and she deposited her butt on the big, upholstered side stool. I pointed to the tray. "Eat."

Her annoyed pout didn't hide the sparkle in her eyes. It wasn't hard to miss that she enjoyed my company. Again, I slid the thought to the side and took up my seat across from her at the little table and reached for the orange juice.

We ate in silence. I poured us each the last of the coffee, then put everything but our cups on the tray and placed it outside the door again. I took up my place across the table and began.

"I think we both know you have to leave here. The question is, when."

"You have some paperwork I have to sign?"

"Yes, I do." I retrieved the envelope with the documents she needed to acknowledge marked in red arrows. I pulled my stool around, laid the papers out on the table before us, one by one, and explained what she was accepting.

"You can, of course, request that all this be liquidated, and we can send you a check, or you can leave it all invested as John had it set up. Or...you can think about it for a few days or weeks or whatever. That's what I'd recommend. Not to do anything now. Just let things sit until everything settles. John's estate will handle all the fees. And his attorney can explain things better than I can, but you should get your own advisor and attorney now."

"I can't use you?"

"Yes, you can. But right now, I represent the estate. And that's why I think you should sign everything to leave it all intact for now. And then rearrange things when you get back home and situated."

"Okay. That sounds good to me." She retrieved a purple, felt-tipped pen from her purse, and I stopped her.

"No. I need black ink, please. Here." I handed her one of my pens.

She read the barrel with her eyebrows raised. "Very official."

I leaned back in my chair, starting to get antsy. She still wasn't taking the paperwork seriously. But, she brought her eyes down to the top paper and squinted.

"Where do I sign?"

I leaned over and pointed. She leaned closer and signed her name, then looked up at me, her sparkling azure eyes making my mouth water. I'd not noticed how blue they were, or how golden and soft her hair was, or how nice it would be to push those golden strands to the side and kiss her neck.

I moved back, setting my spine straight.

She handed me the top paper, and I placed it in the envelope Roger had provided. "And here?" she raised her eyebrows, begging for me to show her again. I knew it was a ruse, but I participated anyway.

"There."

She signed, and this time, I didn't move when our faces were so close our lips nearly touched. "Is it okay if I kiss my advisor? Can you help me with this feeling I have about wanting to kiss you, Sean?"

I hesitated, and she took it as a sign I would let her. Just before she bridged the gap, I leaned back again.

"That's not a good idea, Ariel. I'm here to do one specific job."

"And you've done your job well. Can't a girl say thank you?"

I was in pain. My dick was about three sizes too large for my pants, despite what I was willing to admit to myself. She was the tethered one flying in the wind, and I was the one who held the string. If I let go, I'd fly off with her, and we'd be lost. I could tell that much already.

"I have to focus on getting you home safely."

"What if I don't want to be safe, Sean?" Her eyes pulled me in, underpinning my firm resolve. "Just a little danger-ous—" she said as she leaned in to me, "kiss. Just one, Sean. A thank you kiss."

And then her lips were on mine. Her tongue pressed its way into my mouth. I inhaled her breaths, her scent, her little moan when our tongues touched. My pulse was running wild, and I could feel the dull ache and need for a woman who I knew would be very good to me. I had to stop it.

She grabbed my hand and placed it on her chest, then slid it under the fabric of the dress easily. "Don't stop, Sean. Just a few minutes of dangerous indulgence. Let's pretend this is the meal we wanted for the rest of our lives, and this is the first bite."

She was on my lap in an instant, pulsing her hips and rubbing her sex up and down the hardness of my ridge. Her fingers explored my face, my neck. Her hot mouth opened, drawing me in.

I wanted to get up, but she pressed against me. "Please," she whispered in my ear. "Let me say thank you."

My hand squeezed her breast, and I heard her hiss between her teeth. I adjusted my hips, and her fingers undid my zipper quickly, drawing me out. Up and down she moved her fingers around my shaft, fingering the sensitive tip while she licked her lips and stared into my eyes.

"Do you feel how grateful I am, Sean?"

I wanted to snicker, but she squeezed me harder and then reached down and took my balls, too.

I finally gave her the serious, yearning look of a man in pain, one who might die if he didn't get inside her that instant. I lifted her until the tip of my cock was pressing against her wet lips, and then pulled her down on me, hard. She arched her back, then undulated and moved against me, rising and falling in a gentle stroke that almost drove me over the edge. Somewhere, I screamed at myself to hold back, but then there was the incredible way she felt, the softness and curves of her body, the kisses, and press of flesh against flesh as she rode me, her knees at my thighs on the stool.

I removed her dress to marvel at the way her breasts looked as we moved together. I tasted her sweet nipples.

Suddenly, I picked her up and brought her into the bedroom. Her legs wrapped around me as I crawled onto the bed and laid her down. I took her wrists in one hand and placed her arms over her head, holding her left butt cheek up so I could get deep and press into her again and again, forcing myself to move against her inner channel.

Our lovemaking lasted longer than I thought possible, each kiss driving me crazy with need again, the new places explored sending me to greater heights. She kept right with me, and then I let go of the string and let her fly. Her orgasm was a true thing of beauty. I reveled in her surprise, then in her wonder as her muscles worked against mine, and then in the graceful sigh as she came back down to Earth. In her simmering satisfaction, I filled her with everything I had.

CHAPTER 27

So much for restraint and decorum, I thought while I kissed the peach mounds of her ass, rubbing my finger up and down her butt crack and then burying it in her channel from behind, pushing her nub with my other fingers and making her rear rise up and quiver. I loved that ass. I could love her little body for two days straight and never eat or sleep, that's how much I needed this type of connection. I'd never had it before. I was lost again.

I knew it was wrong as I hoisted her hips up, putting her on all fours on her knees. I replaced my finger with my tongue, and she gasped for air.

"You okay, baby?"

"Yes. No, don't stop!"

"I'm not going to, honey. I'm afraid I only have one switch. And right now, it's on, sweetheart."

I sucked her juices. She clutched the sheets beneath her, pressing her tailbone into my face. I rose to my knees, hovering over her, placing my cock at her opening again, which was swollen and most likely sore. "Sorry, baby, but I gotta come inside you again." She jerked as I went full in.

We were wiping out the whole day. My phone went off. I heard the pings of texts. She asked me if I should get those calls, I told her, "next time. I'll stop in a little bit," except we didn't. On and on it went until I took her to the shower and we fucked there, too.

As we parted, allowing the warm water to sluice down our bodies, we began to laugh. I'd never met anyone like her before, and doubted I ever would again.

"Ariel, I think you should come with a warning tag. Seriously. I can't get enough."

"You're not supposed to. I'm the same way."

We gave each other a serious kiss, and I placed my forehead against hers. The water was still running.

"Well, I guess it's back to the real world."

"Do we have to?"

"Yes, unless we want this to be the last day of our lives. Let's see if we can make it last at least a week, okay?" I showed her a mocking face as if she were a complete idiot and I was, too.

And we were. I'd done exactly what I told myself I wouldn't do, shouldn't do. And now I'd have to deal with the consequences. But it had been important to be with her, to get right with her, to be cemented forever in her heart. We had to connect. It was as necessary as breathing.

She giggled and twirled in my arms then brushed her face with the warm water and started to get out of the shower.

I put my arm around her torso. "Ariel," I said to her ear. "You can't leave me now. I can't let you go."

She smiled and turned her head up to receive another kiss. "Are you kidnapping me?"

"I am. I'm dragging you to my bed, and you're not going to leave."

She rolled her head back as I kissed her neck. My right hand traveled down her front, finding her moist folds intoxicating again.

"I am ruined. No kidding, sweetheart."

She closed the stall door and pressed her slippery, warm body against mine again. "This is the way you're supposed to feel when you find paradise. It isn't an island. Not something you can buy. But this is the adventure I was looking for, Sean. Now that you've taken me there, I don't want to be anywhere else."

"Stay with me in New York. I can't let you go to California."

"I'll consider everything as long as you are beside me."

It was nearly two o'clock when my shriveled body exited the shower. We'd used up so much water, I was wondering if the hotel would send a maintenance crew.

I carefully put on my clothes as I watched her put her dress back on. I reached for my cell phone and felt how heavy it now seemed. My real world calling me back.

I sat on the stool, and she wrapped her arms around me from behind while I scrolled through the messages.

Stephanie had gotten frosty. Sal had called. Nothing else was important except the flight times. I knew Ariel saw everything over my shoulder. "I asked to have some times researched for us."

"Who's Stephanie?"

"My boss's assistant. No one you have to worry about."

She resumed her place on her stool and scanned the paperwork scattered on the table and on the floor.

I helped her gather them together again. "We'd better get the rest of these done. I'm going to send them to Roger. I don't want to risk losing them."

"You're going to trust the mail?"

"I think it would be safer than on our person, don't you?"

She was quiet. Then she sighed. "Let's get this done, Sean. And then let's put all this danger behind us. I don't want to worry about anything ever again."

I laughed and then tempered it when I saw her face. "The world isn't like that. We had a few beautiful hours of distraction, Ariel. But now we have to make a plan and stick to it."

She nodded. "I have faith in you."

"It's gonna be both of us working this out."

I explained the choices on flights. I told her we could go over all the trust information when we got to New York. We didn't have to decide anything else right now except our escape route.

"And I want to get one thing done first. I need to get this mailed." I held up the package pre-addressed to Roger. "I'll go downstairs and be right back up, okay?"

"Don't leave me."

"I have to get this posted."

"Let's do it on the way out. I don't want you to leave me alone. Not until we're home."

I chuckled. "Okay. So we can take the red-eye tonight, or wait until tomorrow. It looks like they have three choices for times."

"Red-eye. That's the first one, right?"

"Yup."

"That's the one I want. We fly to New York?"

"Yes, ma'am. I'm texting Stephanie right now."

Stephanie texted back *done* and then, *Roger will pick you up at the airport. Gotta meet the girl.* I texted her back a heart and a pirate face with a patch over one eye.

Ariel stood up and put her hands to her mouth. "Oh, no!"

I looked up. "What?"

"My passport. It's at the hotel."

"Where, in your room?"

"Yes, in the side of the suitcase, or I might have—" She stopped to think about it. "Unless—" She started to rummage through her purse and sat back down. "I don't have it. We'll have to go back there."

I didn't like it one bit. But that was the hand we were dealt.

"Then we go get it."

I got another frosty text from Stephanie asking for Ariel's name. I responded, and soon got confirmation that everything was paid for and would be waiting for us at the airport. We were to be there by ten for the midnight flight home. I texted her back.

I owe you the biggest, most handsome pirate in all the Caribbean. No one comes close to being right for you yet. It will take extensive research, but I'll find you one, and it will be worth the wait.

She responded: *Promises promises. Just get back here in one piece. Sal's worried.*

We picked up the room, repacked my bag with Ariel's things, and left down the service elevator again. In the lobby, we quickly entered the business center and spoke to a young, attractive clerk, who took our package, which cost me over a hundred dollars. "But it will get there day after tomorrow. Guaranteed."

The lobby was busy with new check-ins. I corralled a bellboy to get us a cab for the airport but told them to meet us at the side entrance at the laundry. He gave me a strange look but agreed. In five minutes, we were loaded and headed east to the airport.

I gave him the name of Ariel's hotel, and we arrived less than a half-hour later. It was nearing five o'clock. We had plenty of time. "I need for you to wait for us a few minutes while we go inside and get something."

He agreed.

The reception desk was staffed with six clerks. We rushed past them to the elevators. I surveyed the room quickly and didn't see anyone who took special notice of us, but I had a strange feeling we were not out of danger yet.

On the tenth floor, Ariel led us to the number written on her room key card. The light turned green, and we heard the latch release. I sighed in relief. We were that much closer to getting home.

Inside, the room had been ransacked. Lamps were overturned, all the sheets were off the bed, and the mattress was tossed. Ariel's clothes were strewn all over the floor. Her suitcase lay open-mouthed in the corner. I ran and picked it up, searching the pockets.

She was looking for something else on the floor. Beside her bed was a book, a romance novel. She bent, picked up the title, and spread it open to reveal her passport still tucked inside.

"My bookmark to the life of my dreams!" she said as she held it up.

"You want to take your things? We have time."

She handed me items to put inside the case, and I dutifully folded and arranged them. We took her lucky romance book, as well. She added her toiletries bag from the bathroom and double-checked the drawers and closets. "That's it."

I latched the case, and we were out in the hallway in seconds. We heard voices coming from around the corner, so we ducked into the stairwell, closing the door carefully without a sound, and started jogging down the steps for two floors, then found an elevator and rode down the rest of the way.

Our driver was nowhere to be seen. There was a bell stand that was unmanned, and it made me nervous. I grabbed Ariel's hand, and we ran to the first taxi in line over the objection of several other cabs behind him.

As we pulled out onto the roadway heading to the airport, I saw another vehicle exit the hotel and follow us. I asked the driver to speed up, but the car behind was nearly on our tail in minutes.

Crossing the road all of a sudden was a large, open-air delivery van full of live chickens. Our driver slammed on his brakes, but I knew it was no use. The cab swerved, its right rear fishtailing. I knew we'd hit the van broadside as I watched the faces of dozens of chickens witnessing our cab heading straight for them. In a screech of tires and the crunch of metal and glass, the impact left me with one last view of Ariel's lovely face, white chicken feathers floating around and sticking in her hair like stardust.

And then everything went black.

CHAPTER 28

I woke up with Ariel leaning over me. "Sean, are you all right?" She was moving my face from side to side, tears and blood streaming down her cheeks. I felt something warm beneath me, and as I began to gain consciousness, realized I was on the paved road—pulled or thrown from the car.

I tried to ask her if she was hurt, but I couldn't talk. I couldn't breathe. I gasped and heard her say, "Oh my God. We're losing him! Somebody help me!"

A huge weight was on my chest, making breath impossible. I hit my chest with my hand, and someone pulled Ariel up by one arm.

"Mum, he cannot breathe. You smotherin' da man."

Her shocked expression shot through her face right before she burst into tears.

"Oh, I've killed him."

I tried to get up, say something. Loving hands pushed me gently back down. I needed to cough. Turning my head to the right, I was able to inhale, and just before expelling some phlegm, I came face-to-face with a curious, white hen, who had crept between dark and dusty legs of all shapes and sizes.

There was no blood on my tongue, and as I inhaled again, I didn't feel any pain. Grateful that I apparently didn't have any broken ribs, I began moving other parts of me. My feet and ankles moved, as did my upper legs and knees. My fingers could grip, except the index finger on my left hand was bent and had a cut with blood running down the side.

A crowd began to develop. Ariel dropped to her knees again.

"Sean, I'm so sorry I was pushing on you. I just—"

"No worries. I survived." I gave her a crooked grin as I leaned on my elbow. Several people in the audience sighed, and there was a mixture of claps and pidgin English with words laced in like "miracle" and "he's a fit yank," and other terms.

"You get up slowly and don' be pushin' things too hard," an authoritarian woman barked at me, and I took her word for it, allowing several strong arms to help me to a standing position.

I was taller than most of the crowd, so it didn't take long to survey the damage. Our driver was sitting by the side of the road with a bloody rag pressed to his forehead, speaking wildly with his other arm adding emphasis. The delivery van had tipped on its side, falling away from the crash impact, but enough chickens had survived that children and one dog were chasing them all over the road. A line of traffic had backed up, and the people were starting to honk. The crowd continued to grow, people naturally curious about the whole affair.

Behind several other vehicles, I saw the dark car that had followed us. For now, they stayed put. The driver's-side window was down, and a man's arm rested on the ledge.

I put my arm around Ariel and whispered in her ear, "We have to get to the airport quick. I don't want to be taken to a hospital, and I don't want to deal with the local police."

"Gotcha. Let me see what I can do." She started to walk away, and I grabbed her arm.

"Stay close, and avoid that black car that was following us."

She started to turn to look for it, but I grabbed her and planted a big kiss on her lips, nearly sending her crashing to the ground. I got more small applause and lots of whistles of approval.

"Whoa. I guess you are going to be okay." She gave me a dreamy smile and a wink and started to work the crowd.

A huge hand gripped my shoulder and squeezed so hard I thought the bad guys had employed Shrek.

"Sean, my man!"

I knew who it was partly by the voice, and partly by the shadow that his body cast over me. I allowed his hand to turn my body as if I were a cardboard stick figure.

"Cecil. What a surprise. You following me, too?"

"No, man, just dropped some bodies off at de airport. Why you not call me?"

"We tried to. But...it's a long story."

Ariel came to my side, and I smiled to think she thought to defend me. It was a cute gesture.

"Everything working okay?"

"Everything but this." I demonstrated my odd-angled finger.

"Sean, who is this man?"

"This is the driver who brought me to Nelson's Bay on my first day." I looked between him and Ariel. "Cecil, this is Ariel. Ariel, Cecil."

"I am enchanted!" Instead of shaking her hand, he pulled her into his big chest that was mostly belly and squeezed her so tightly she crossed her eyes at me. Again, I had to stifle a laugh.

"So, dis is no place for a catch-up. We got cars all over and...Oh. My. God. Somebody's losing some chickens."

My hands were bloody from the little cuts I'd received from the broken glass. But sure enough, everything else was fine. Ariel kept insisting that she was unhurt. We had both worn our seatbelts.

"Cecil, can you take us to the airport?"

"I got another fare coming up."

"I'll give you $400," I whispered.

His eyes took notice. "I'm going to give dat odder fare to my cousin. You two come with me."

"Cecil, you need to get our bags out of the car. Show him, Ariel."

He had to kick in the rear passenger side door, nearly folding it back on itself, but then, with his massive hands, he ripped the door off its hinges. I was seriously impressed. Ariel showed him the bags, and he was able to extricate them both. Ariel's square suitcase was shaped more like a five-sided cube.

"You gonna need another one of these, and my auntie sells them. Imagine that." Cecil smiled his wide grin, and it was then I noticed he had a gold front tooth with a dollar sign inlaid there.

"Why, you old capitalist. As long as we can get to the airport well before ten. If you get us there before eight, I'll throw in another hundred."

He grabbed the bags and shouted over his shoulder, "Follow me."

I addressed the crowd behind me. "Show's over, folks." I heard the sirens arriving and added, "The police are here to help untangle this mess."

I jogged to catch up with Ariel and Cecil, who nearly gunned the motor before I had a chance to sit down. I fell into Ariel, who was already strapped in. I glanced behind us and could not make out a single form, as the entire rear view window was filled with a rolling storm of red clay.

"You sure you're okay?" I asked Ariel.

"You've asked me ten times already, Sean." She lowered her voice, "You sure you have enough cash for all of this?"

"Not your concern, but the answer is yes. Still, you'll owe me."

As I strapped in, she snuggled against me. "Promises, promises."

There was a tiny convenience mall before the main entrance to the airport. As with everywhere on the island, adjacent to it were open-air storefronts with corrugated roofs.

"Cecil, I mean it about getting to the airport early."

"Not a problem, man. This will only take two seconds. Da lady needs a new bag, and Auntie has just the right one for her."

I was beginning to feel stiff and knew there would be bruises showing up soon. I couldn't wait to get into the lounge seats and take a restorative catnap, once I knew we were safely headed home to New York. Until then, I had to stay on high alert. I opened the door, disentangled myself from the rear seat, and drew Ariel with me.

Cecil had taken the liberty of grabbing Ariel's bag. "Auntie, we have a problem here, and I think you can fix it."

They vocalized pidgin back and forth, Cecil erupting in a belly laugh as his "auntie" slapped his arm.

"Come on in, child. I have just whatever you like. First quality."

She had an assortment of old, red and blue Samsonite suitcases that might have been new ten years ago. Some hard cases had Disney characters. I pointed to the red one with the marijuana leaf on the outside, and Ariel shook her head. She stopped in front of a red hard case covered with little white hearts. "This one."

Auntie opened it up, showing her the satin-lined pockets and the extra key that went with it.

"Fine. We'll take it. I reached for my wallet and held it close.

"Sir. You got tomato sauce all over your shirt. You need another shirt to take this fine lady out to dinner with."

She was right, of course. And so I was forced to buy another ugly blue-and-turquoise-flowered shirt with hula girls on it made in Malaysia.

"This is island fabric. Made here," she informed me, but I didn't argue.

Ariel pointed to a halter top dress made of the same fabric. "Can I have that one?"

What could I say? I was lost. Hopelessly lost. I pulled out a wad of bills and paid the woman. She threw in a couple of bottles of water for the two-minute trip to the airport, so I gave one to Cecil.

"We'll share."

He delivered us to the United gate at a quarter to eight, earning his extra hundred dollars. Ariel had already transferred her contents to the new suitcase, so we left her old one behind. Like a couple of newlyweds, we bade Cecil good-bye, and I paid him extra, which earned me a belly hug just like Ariel had gotten.

"You come back to our peaceful, beautiful island. We'll all still be here waiting for you." His grin and gold tooth reminded me that if I were really, really stupid, I'd come back and see him again.

Of all the things I'd say about this trip to beautiful Paradise, if it ever really did exist, I would never call it peaceful. Dangerous or passionate? I'd have to say yes. But peaceful? A walk in Central Park would be peaceful. Having a drink and watching the people rushing to get to work, or an espresso in the early morning after my run. Now, that was peaceful.

No one was lurking at or around the ticket counter, and our first-class boarding passes were issued. We parted to use the restrooms to freshen up and walked out from opposite walls at the exact same time with our matching clothes.

"This one goes to the homeless in Manhattan along with the red one."

"Sean. It matches mine."

"Don't remind me."

Customs was filled with sweaty men looking official. I noticed their crisply starched white, short-sleeved shirts and epaulettes, unlike what I knew our US customs officials wore. The handsome government worker positioned his stamp with great care, and we were admitted to the security screening without a question being asked. But he did add, "Nice shirt."

We made it through security, and I finally began to relax as we approached the gate. Of course, with Ariel, a planeful of terrorists could arrive at any time on the runway and start shooting up things, so I reserved enough energy to stay alert.

We sat and had a drink. Ariel had a coconut cocktail, and mine was mostly pineapple juice, but it tasted delicious.

The plane's first-class section was huge and contained large sleeper seats that could be separated by a curtain. We put our luggage overhead and sat back in the cool, blue leather, waiting for the rest of the plane to load and to begin our run home. We both had the rum punch this time since I figured it was finally safe, and Roger would be picking us up.

We clinked glasses when we were served, and I started to become one with the seat.

"You know, Sean, we didn't really decide what we were going to do next."

"What do you mean?"

"Well, I can stay with you a few days, and you can show me New York City. But after that?"

I leaned over to her, planted a kiss, and whispered, "Why don't you just stay in New York?"

"But what about our great adventure?"

I wasn't sure I was hearing her very well. I winced and asked, "Ariel, we just had—"

"Our plans. Our strategy."

"Ariel, our strategy was to get off the island alive."

"But when are we going back? We have to make plans."

"Go back? You said you didn't want to—"

"But you're here now. You can protect me. Suddenly all these adventures keep coming up, things that never could have happened before. Sean, you said I was a wealthy woman."

"If you're careful, your money will last your whole life. Enough to perhaps leave something behind for someone."

"You will still be my advisor?"

"I love advising you." I turned on my side, but I could feel some stiffness in my hip, so I adjusted my knee to take the pressure off. "Especially in the middle of the afternoon. I'd like to see what you look like all tied up in my bed. I could advise you on what you could do to earn your freedom, kiss by kiss."

A woman in the seat across the aisle leaned forward to examine my state of mind.

"Hold me for ransom?"

"Sort of." I searched her pretty face. "Ariel, if you'll let me, I'd just like to spend my time making you the happiest woman alive. We don't have to make any commitments yet—"

"Oh! But I want to. Everything is possible if you're there."

I held her chin between my thumb and two fingers, drawing her face to mine as I kissed her. "I want to be Mr. Ariel. That suits me just fine, too."

"Good. Then it's settled."

I had already started leaning back in my seat as the plane started to taxi. I knew I should not ask what she meant. I was good with a wedding, a life of forever with Ariel, knowing full well I'd probably be spending most of my time keeping her out of trouble. But that was what I was good at. And I'd love every minute of it.

But I had a feeling I wasn't going to like this.

"So, tell me what's settled."

"I want a big wedding, lasting a week long, on my island. On *our* island. I want all our friends to come and spend a week with us, celebrating. We'll have campfires and feasts, erect beautiful tents like they do in India, hunt for buried treasure and dance all night long under the stars. We'll play just as the pirates of old did. We'll all go skinny-dipping under the moon. I want to build a house there, Sean, a place off the grid. With you by my side, I feel safe. Live private, where no one can find us."

I wondered how I could be so incredibly lucky and so incredibly fucked at the same time.

"Tell me you're in for it all, Sean."

I swallowed and then just had to throw my head back to laugh.

"Anything you want, sweetheart."

I hope you have enjoyed *Paradise-In Search of Love.* There will be a further adventure when Sean and Ariel go back to the island in search of buried treasure, the wedding you won't want to miss, and all that could go wrong in the meantime. Look for this new drama sometime early 2018.

If you enjoyed this story, please consider leaving a review at: http://authorsharonhamilton.com/in-search-of-love.php

ABOUT THE AUTHOR

NYT and USA Today best-selling author Sharon Hamilton's award-winning Navy SEAL Brotherhood series have been a fan favorite from the day the first one was released. They've earned her the coveted Amazon author ranking of #1 in Romantic Suspense, Military Romance and Contemporary Romance categories, as well as in Gothic Romance for her Vampires of Tuscany and Guardian Angels. Her characters follow a sometimes rocky road to redemption through passion and true love.

Her Golden Vampires of Tuscany are not like any vamps you've read about before, since they don't go to ground and can walk around in the full light of the sun.

Her Guardian Angels struggle with the human charges they are sent to save, often escaping their vanilla world of Heaven for the brief human one. You won't find any of these beings in any Sunday school class.

She lives in Sonoma County, California with her husband and two Dobermans. A lifelong organic gardener, when she's not writing, she's getting *verra verra* dirty in the mud, or wandering Farmers Markets looking for new Heirloom varieties of vegetables and flowers.

She loves hearing from her fans:
Sharonhamilton2001@gmail.com

Her website is: www.authorsharonhamilton.com
Find out more about Sharon, her upcoming releases,
appearances and news from her newsletter:
www.authorsharonhamilton.com/contact.php#mailing-list

Facebook: facebook.com/SharonHamiltonAuthor
Twitter: twitter.com/sharonlhamilton
Pinterest: pinterest.com/AuthorSharonH
Google Plus: plus.google.com/u/1/+SharonHamiltonAuthor/posts
Youtube: youtube.com/channel/
UCDInkxXFpXp_4Vnq08ZxMBQ
Soundcloud: soundcloud.com/sharon-hamilton-1
BookBub: bookbub.com/authors/sharon-hamilton
Rockin' Romance Readers: facebook.com/groups/
sealteamromance
Goodreads Group: goodreads.com/group/
show/199125-sharon-hamilton-readers-group
Online Store: sharon-hamilton-author.myshopify.com

Join Sharon's Review Teams:
eBook Reviews: reviewcrewsh@gmail.com
Audio Reviews: reviewcrewaudio@gmail.com

Life is one fool thing after another.
Love is two fool things after each other.

SHARON HAMILTON'S BOOK LIST

SEAL BROTHERHOOD SERIES
SEAL Encounter (Book .5)
Accidental SEAL (Book 1)
SEAL Endeavor (Book 1.5)
Fallen SEAL Legacy (Book 2)
SEAL Under Covers (Book 3)
SEAL The Deal (Book 4)
Cruisin' For A SEAL (Book 5)
SEAL My Destiny (Book 6)
SEAL Of My Heart (Book 7)

BAD BOYS OF SEAL TEAM 3 SERIES
SEAL's Promise (Book 1)
SEAL My Home (Book 2)
SEAL's Code (Book 3)

BAND OF BACHELORS SERIES
Lucas (Book 1)
Alex (Book 2)
Jake (Book 3)
Jake2 (Book 4)

TRUE BLUE SEALS SERIES
True Navy Blue (prequel to Zak)
Zak (Includes novella above)

NASHVILLE SEAL SERIES
Nashville SEAL (Book 1)
Nashville SEAL: Jameson (Books 1 & 2 combined)

AUDIOBOOKS
All of Sharon Hamilton's books are available as audiobooks narrated by J.D. Hart.

REVIEWS